The stars show themselves.
by CJ Kennedy.

The stars show themselves.
by CJ Kennedy.

Eye Publishing.

Oklahoma City. Oklahoma.

Copyright 2021

Eye Publishing

All Rights Reserved.

No part of this book may be reproduced by any mechanical, photographic, or electronic process, or in the form of a phonographic recording; nor may it be stored in a retrieval system, transmitted, or otherwise copied for public or private use—other than for "fair use" as brief quotations embodied in articles and reviews—without prior written permission of the author/publisher. This is a work of fiction. the characters, names, incidents, dialogue, and locales are works from the author's imagination or are places used fictitiously. Any resemblance to people living or dead is purely coincidental, except as stated in the author's note.

ISBN-13: 978-0578844343
Cover design: CJ Kennedy

The stars show themselves.

Prologue. Richvill, 2130. 8

Chapter one. Welcome to Richvill aka hell. 12

Chapter two. Want homophobia? Go to Flormorent School for ages k-12. 24

Chapter three. When a funeral happens. 38

Chapter four. When you have to do a truth serum assignment and get locked in the car. 52

Part Two. A few things go wrong and more about Rachel. What will happen to Dylan and Maxton? 80

Chapter five. So, are you prepared for a Rachel takeover? 82

Chapter six. Rachel is a badass revolutionary. 96

Chapter seven. Losing your voice! And the first step of the rebellion. 110

Chapter eight. You know that feeling that the world's ending? Well, for Rachel, it may be. Do revolutionaries have to go to school? 124

Chapter nine. Dylan's back, and he's in on the plan. Also, Rachel can be a jerk. 138

Chapter ten. A war is brewing. Dylan is coming. 152

Chapter eleven. Rachel's grief

and the rebellion. Also, the crying person. 166

Chapter twelve. The walkout and the rebellion. 180

Author note. 194

About the author. 196

Prologue. Richvill, 2130.

A boy ran through the forest. His hair was slightly brown, and he had black eyes. He was a dark blur. His black eyes shone in the woods. It started raining. His hands went clammy. He watched as trees swayed back and forth.

"Maxton!" the boy yelled, not angered—just scared. His heart pounded as he reached towards absolutely nothing. The boy tensed up and screamed, "Maxton! Please come out! I need to talk to you! Please!" He screamed the words, sobbing. His throat hurt. Then, he heard a shuffle.

"Dylan?" A similar voice called out. He had a sing-song voice, one that made anyone's heart pound, a recognizable voice one that could comfort the sobbing, He needed that comfort more than anything. Maxton carefully moved out from behind a tree, his black hair curled up. He had brown eyes and thin shoulders.

"I'm here," he said running towards Dylan, hugging him. His arms carefully wrapped around the boy.

"I thought you were killed," Dylan whispered.

"No, I don't think anyone knows," Maxton whispered, pulling away from Dylan. That's when the two boys heard it, a click of a camera. The two boys froze. Their hearts stopped in their chests when Maxton whispered, "They won't know about us."

"What was that?" Dylan asked, scanning the whole woods. That's when he saw them, a boy with golden brown hair. wearing a red shirt with grey pants, holding a camera, He looked over Maxton and Dylan. Hatred bored a hole into them.

"Fags," the golden brown-haired boy whispered before running off.

Dylan and Maxton remained still, too shocked to move, too shocked to think, too shocked to breathe, or even think. They both knew the danger of being together in their town, but they never thought this would happen. Now, that person had a picture.

"Blackmail," Dylan closed his eyes for a second, his eyes shaking. He reopened them to see Maxton.

Chapter one. Welcome to Richvill aka hell.

"Hey, it's okay. It's not that bad We look like two friends talking in the woods," Maxton said, looking over Dylan. Tears were flooding Dylan's eyes, threatening to spill over. He was breathing hard. Tears stung his cheeks as Maxton ran over to hug him.

"Listen, it's gonna be fine," he whispered. rubbing Dylan's brown curly hair. He was shaking like a leaf. It felt more like a dream, but Dylan knew it wasn't.

"What if he took more pictures of us that we don't know about?" Dylan asked, fear wrapping around him, melting him like acid, a terrible painful sensation. He let out a deep breath.

"We'll be ok," Maxton whispered, touching Dylan's face. Dylan wanted to believe what

Maxton was saying, but he couldn't. He was beyond reasoning. Tears spilled over Dylan's face. He fell to the ground, as wind slowly brushed his hair to the side, He couldn't breathe. He just started crying. Maxton promptly sat on his knees, rubbing Dylan's back. Maxton wanted to be strong for Dylan, for his own sake. Maxton carefully wrapped an arm around Dylan.

"Take a deep breath. Hold it," he whispered. Dylan inhaled, still shaking. He never had been this scared in his 15 years of existence. He was finally able to calm down after a while.

The sun had started going down, so the forest got darker as the realization of going home scared him. If his parents found out, they'd disown him, but Dylan knew if he didn't come home, they would be suspicious. He said goodbye to Maxton. He walked out of the forest, took a deep breath, and slipped his hands into his jeans. He looked at the ground, watching his feet move one foot in front of the other. He noticed how his left leg moved inwards when he took a deep breath. Then, he looked around him, being met with the only Walmart in town, the familiar blue sign, and right next to Walmart was the town's only McDonalds. Dylan lived in the red and brown bricked house next to McDonald's, a one-story house with stone beams, holding up a hood covering the porch. Dylan climbed the steps before digging in his pocket for the key, then, slowly pushing the key in the hole and twisting it, he entered the house. A young girl with red curly hair looked up at him. She was wearing a blue dress. She ran towards him.

"Dylan! You're home!" she cried happily.

"Hey, Katherine," he whispered, smiling at his little sister.

"Mom and Dad want to talk to you!" she said happily. Dylan's body shook.

Shit, he thought to himself, slowly walking towards the dining room. His mother was standing in the kitchen. She was wearing a red shirt and black jeans. She was cooking dinner. His dad was sitting at the dining room table. He was sitting with his arms crossed on the table.

"Son, sit down," his dad said. His face was like cardboard. He looked at his eyes. They seemed so dead. He had a paper in his right hand. Dylan's eyes shook.

"Yes. Sir," Dylan said, sliding in his seat.

"On Monday, 10:30pm, Veronica Arabia was found dead in her own bed. She committed suicide," his dad explained, looking at his son. Dylan sat there, his hands rolled into fists.

"We have reasons that this was for attention," his mother chimed in from the kitchen. Dylan's rage filled his head.

"She wrote something for you," his dad said, handing him a one-slip journal page, Dylan reached towards the page, pulling it closer to him. He started reading it.

Dear Dylan,

I don't know how to start this letter, but here I go.

I just wanted to say, I'm so sorry, I just couldn't anymore. While looking into the mirror, seeing someone I'm not, being told I was going through a phase, that I was too young to know anything about myself, saying I just wanted attention.

Do you remember that night, when me and you had a sleepover? I woke up crying.

And I said, I was fine.

Dylan couldn't read the note. He pushed it away, sobbing. Was it his fault? Why wasn't he there for him more? Did he do anything?

"Son, it's not your fault. She was just imitating kids from the city," his father said, reaching his arm and resting his hand on his shoulder.

"He wasn't like that, Father! And you knew that," Dylan snapped. He hated how much he had cried that day.

"Feelings of wanting to die are only felt by adults," his dad said.

Dylan stood up and left his chair, pushing it in before running into his room and pushing the brown door open. sitting on the bed. The realization started sinking in. He looked around his room. He looked around the room until his eyes fell on his phone, He reached out for the red box, slowly turning it over as he read the contact name.

"Von." He clicked on the text message.

"I'm sorry, Dylan."

That was the last text message. He looked at it, before typing in.

"Why? Did you do this? I'm sorry I wasn't there." Dylan typed. He closed his eyes for a second.

Today hadn't been an easy day. Neither was yesterday or the week before. In Richvill, there was never an easy day for children, teenagers or adults who were part of the LGBTQ+ community.

That was why, if anyone saw those pictures, Dylan and Maxton would be killed, possibly literally. That was what pushed Von into suicide: the hatred of that town, spreading like a disease. Dylan looked at the ground. His eyes burned from crying, but he couldn't sleep. He stared at his phone, too emotionally tired to feel anything. He wasn't hungry. He sat on his bed. Katherine came in and fell asleep on his lap,

When it was around 12:50am, Dylan fell asleep sitting up. His phone was on the charger. Dylan hardly moved the whole night. Katherine slept in her own room. An alarm clock sounded, waking up Dylan.

He forced his eyes open, hearing soldiers sweeping the street.

Dylan, pulled his black button-up around his

shoulders, buttoning it up, pushing himself off the bed. Walking over to his closet, he grabbed his blue jeans and his gold belt. He tucked his shirt in and tightened his belt. He didn't want to go to school without Von. The thought of being outed at school scared him. Right now, the only thing keeping him going was the thought of when he turned 18, he could leave Richvill forever.

Dylan walked down the light blue. painted hallways.

"Son, are you hungry?" his mother asked from the kitchen.

"No, ma'am," Dylan replied, walking out the door, sighing. He always wondered what happened to make Richvill go so wrong. He walked towards the small school. His arms were in his Jean pockets, as looked over the yellow and brown bricked school. A bell hung from the front. He slowly stepped up the stairs. Each step became harder as he saw the place he and Von always met. He could practically see him.

He had a small button nose, along with stormy grey eyes and wore the school uniform pink dress. His red curly hair stuck out from underneath a grey beanie. Dylan already felt tears in his eyes forming, but he forced them back down, like some sort of gag. It was the second suicide in nine months. He hated it. Every single part of him hated it.

And the thing that happened was, all kids would have to stand up in front of the whole class and explain why Von wouldn't be at school. He didn't want to, but he had to. For the school's sake, he pushed the door open, going to his locker, rubbing his hand through his brown hair.

Dylan took off his slippers and pulled out blue sneakers, slipping his feet into them. He looked in his locker mirror. Brown hair frizzed in every direction, left and right. He pulled his fingers through his hair, making himself look calm and collected. His black eyes shook back and forth.

"I've got this, I've got this," he whispered. His breath fogged up the glass.

He slammed his locker shut, walking into his classroom. Thirty desks were lined up and down in a straight line. A speech podium stood in front of the black board. The podium was grey, and you had to stand on the wooden board box. He stood there, shaking. The teacher had grey hair tied in a bun, and her face looked like creases in a piece of folded cardboard. She had yellow glasses and used a walker to move around. She likely would roll over a student's toes if she didn't like them, causing a broken toe. She even did it one time.

"Umm, Ms. Jackie, I have to say something once the class gets in here," Dylan explained, rubbing a hand over the smooth wooden desk.

"What do you have to say?" Ms. Jackie asked.

Her voice sounded like a frog's.

"Vo-Veronica Arabia committed suicide," he explained, as he heard the familiar loud ding of the bell that shook the whole school hallways. Suddenly, students flooded the classroom like a school of fish.

"Okay, Class! Dylan Burr has something to say," she croaked out. Dylan's heart pounded.

"I hate to say this, but Von Arabia committed suicide, He was a victim of this town's hatred, a victim of a dysfunctional family," Dylan began to say but was cut off by Ms. Jackie.

"Enough, Dylan! You're causing a scene," she croaked. Her voice drove Dylan crazy. He wanted to stab her in the head.

Dylan jumped off of his box and headed to his desk.

"Now. class, we will be talking about our President Flormorent." She wrote down Flormorent on the whiteboard. A girl with black curly hair and brown eyes, a small nose, the only mixed girl in the whole school, raised her hand.

"He was elected in 2030, when he made the first law against the LGBTQ+ community in 2031. Any type of same sex relationship shall be greeted with 5 years of imprisonment," she explained.

"You are correct," Ma Jackie replied, writing that down.

Chapter two. Want homophobia? Go to Flormorent School for ages k-12.

Class whizzed by as Dylan went to history. Mr. Kugar had been rumored to be a sex offender. That's probably why Dylan was uneasy in that class. A blind girl named Rachel sat in that class. She was pretty. She had curly blonde hair, light blue eyes, and she was extremely caring and loving. She was friends with Von.

"Hey, Rachel!" Dylan said, jogging up to her. She had a pink cane, which she tapped on the ground.

"Hey, Dylan. I heard about Von. Are you okay?" she asked, while walking forward into class 102.

"Not really. I miss him," Dylan told Rachel. His

voice shook as if he were close to crying again, but he didn't When they got into class, Rachel gave the speech that they learned about the government.

"In 2031, the first solider sweep was done, and why was this done?" Mr. Kugar asked.

Dylan raised his hand nervously. He hated doing this. He was scared at what he was about to say.

"The first solider sweep was performed to intimidate the population and find any same sex relationships."

"Correct, Dylan," Mr. Kugar replied, smiling, revealing yellow, crooked teeth that didn't match his black, greased-back hair and professional suit and tie and blue eyes.

Dylan looked aimlessly around the room. He looked at Maxton and smiled. Maxton smiled back. Then, they instantly looked away from each other. Dylan noticed the golden-haired boy glaring at them, before writhing something on a piece of paper. Then, he threw it, hitting Dylan just above the neck.

"What the--"he whispered to himself, grabbing the paper and slowly unfolding it.

"Meet me behind the school, or your little secret is going to be everywhere."

Dylan let out an annoyed sigh and crumbled the paper back up, then slipped it into his pocket.

The class went by slowly as the third bell went off. Dylan walked out of the classroom. He headed to the doors. He had a feeling this was just a bluff but didn't want to test it. Like his mother said, better safe than sorry. He walked outside as leaves gently blew around him. It was warmer than usual.

Dylan stood there completely engulfed in shadows.

There he was, the golden-haired boy. He stood there, looking into Dylan's black eyes.

"Surprised you came, faggot," he hissed out.

Dylan squeezed his own hand into a fist.

"Yeah, I did. What do you want?" Dylan said, slipping his hand into his pocket. The golden-haired boy looked over him.

"Listen, either you put money in my pockets, so we can afford my mother's medical bills, or these pictures will be on the school-board." He was holding up the grey and black camera.

"What photos do you have that's so incriminating?" Dylan asked. A small amount of uncertainty seeped into his voice.

"I'll show you." The golden-haired boy moved around him, standing behind him. He clicked the back of the camera, revealing photos of the two boys holding hands. He moved his finger sideways, revealing a picture of Dylan and Maxton, their lips wrapped around each other, pulling each other closer.

"Why did you photograph this?" Dylan asked,

biting his lower lip. That was a thought going through his head the whole time.

"Cause it's against the law! Dumbass!" the golden-haired boy screamed.

Dylan sighed.

"How much do you need?" Dylan laid his hand in his pocket, feeling his about-50 dollars.

"800," the golden hair boy replied.

"I'm sorry. Just like you, my family's going through a hard time as well. We can't help."

"But what about these photos?! If you can't pay, these are going to be all over school." The golden-haired boy yelled, stomping on the ground. His face went red, like a toddler throwing a temper tantrum, Dylan forced down a bit of laughter.

"So is blackmailing, so you can get the death penalty, and I'll get five years in prison." Dylan smirked, and he also knew while looking at the camera, he couldn't get those photos out.

"You're gonna go to hell!" The golden-haired boy said.

Dylan laughed, as fear seeped into his heart and mind. Little does Dylan know how naive he was and would cause hell in. 3 2 1.

Dylan felt a strong hand yank him back behind the school. He fell hard on his rear, grass starting to stain his hands.

That's when the golden-brown haired boy, grabbed him by the chin, looking over him, before saying, "Listen here! I can move these pictures online, and you'll get arrested. You hear me? Now, either I'll keep this, and this precious bit of information will get out, and you get arrested, or you pay."

Dylan stood there, starting to get nervous. This felt so surreal that he wanted to laugh. He wanted to pretend this was a dream, that if he just said, "Okay, I'm done," that he would wake up from this dream, but he couldn't.

"And what if you're proven guilty of blackmail? I'll be happy to meet you in prison," Dylan said, smirking. God, he could be such a jerk when he wanted to be. But deep inside, his mind was screaming, *don't be so cocky!*

The golden-haired boy looked over him, before sighing.

"Listen, I understand your mom is sick, If I could help, I would, but we've resorted to eating paint chips at my house. I went to the woods to get some roots for us to eat," Dylan explained. Well, the last part wasn't a lie. At dinner and breakfast, his mom was cooking what was left of their meat. Dylan made a mental note to actually get roots from the woods, but the real reason he even went was for Maxton. They could be there completely alone. In the small town. the belief was the woods had been cursed and those who went in never came out.

Dylan ran out from behind the school. His

heart had begun pounding. Yeah, such a genius move—run away from someone who could possibly blackmail him,

"Nice going, Dylan," he said to himself before whacking himself in the head--not hard. It just sounded really bad, because it was a bony part of his wrist into the skull and would cause some sort of undesirable sound.

Dylan took a few steps forward, as he saw a line of about 30 soldiers weaving around the school. They stood their guns pointed. The sun reflected off of the black leather. Two yellow balls hung from their shirt collars. Dylan looked over at them, confused.

That was when he heard one solider in the middle of the line shout, "Food drops are being delivered! These will be divided evenly between the 100 children here!" She shrieked.

Dylan felt all of his muscles tense at once. He hated yelling. That's when he saw about 45 large cardboard crates lined out in front of him, He felt his stomach growl. He hadn't eaten breakfast, so his family could eat, but now he regretted it. Seeing all this food was so tempting. Then, Ms. Jackie came out, hunched over. She walked, slowly moving. Each step was slow.

"Missy, please give the first box to the boy right here." she croaked out. A cardboard box was set in Dylan's arms. The box was about 50 pounds, and Dylan nearly crumbled under the weight, but he didn't. School was let out early. Dylan felt giddy. His family wouldn't go hungry. Soon, he didn't care about the fact that when he ate, he felt sick to some extent. He didn't care about the pain in his stomach.

He walked up to his one-story house. He pushed the door open with his foot as he set the box on the floor.

"Mother, Father, the soldiers have brought a supply of food." Dylan called out. No response.

Dylan looked around the dining room. The light blue wallpaper in the circular dining room, which was so common in Richvill, made Dylan feel even more at home, He sighed, letting his aching arms drop to his sides. He walked over to the table and saw the letter still lying there, He sucked in his breath. He had to find out what his best friends last words were. He slowly pulled out the brown chair and pushed himself down. His hands shook as he reached for the letter, pulling it to himself. He took a deep breath, then looked down at the paper.

"I'm so sorry, I wasn't there Von," he whispered. Then, he started reading where he left off.

Everyone was saying I was just confused, I want to escape, and maybe you'll be happier without me. I took the final pill, so this will be my last letter.

But the point of this letter is to say I'm sorry. Don't hate me—and one request is for you to keep smiling and fulfill your dream of traveling the world. I'll always be there for you.

Yours forever and always,

Von.

Dylan felt all of his emotions fall out to the floor. He just wanted to reach through the letter and hold hands with his friend.

He curled into a ball, still sitting in that chair. Suddenly, he heard the door open.

"Dylan, what is this?" his mother asked, looking at the cardboard crate.

"Soldiers delivered a crate," he explained, still shaken up from the photos. He let his mom start sorting the food. He walked down the long hallway, shaking like a leaf. He pushed the door open and sat on his bed.

His phone was laying on his bed, He lifted up the red cased box, before scanning through each message.

"Dylan, meet me in the woods." It was from Maxton. Why did he need to talk to him? If it was the picture thing, they would have to break up.

Dylan climbed out the window slowly, then ran down the street into the woods.

Richvill was basically a town of buildings down a long stretch of street, a pitstop for travelers and a good place for a few people to get out the car and take selfies. The town's population was about 200. Everyone knew each other.

These were the thoughts running though Dylan's head as he entered the woods, He was swallowed by darkness. Damp air attached itself to Dylan's hair, lips, and lungs.

"Dylan," Maxton said in his own sing song way. If you didn't know better, you would think he was mocking you.

"Maxton, what's going on?" Dylan asked, leaving a hand on Maxton's shoulder.

"Are you okay? I know about Von, but that's not why I need to talk to you," he explained, pushing his arms around Dylan, hugging him.

"That boy, he knows, so my parents—they're going to tell the church," he whispered. Dylan felt his muscles tense. This only meant one thing: conversation therapy.

Maxton held onto him for a good while. They were breathing slowly. They couldn't leave. They had no clue of the outside world. Such a small community meant it was easy to brain wash, so the only way to stop this was to provoke outrage, but that also meant one boy still had to go into the therapy. They talked for a while before the decision was made.

"I'm sorry. We shouldn't have to talk about this," the curly-haired boy said to the other.

"I love you,'" the brown-haired boy said. His heart was heavy as he left the woods and walked into his house. His breath was shaking as his mother backed into a corner, scared of him. felt a shudder go down his spine.

"You know, about me, don't you?" Dylan said

"Dylan, you're sick. Who taught you to be gay?" his father asked.

"No one, sir," he replied.

His mother started crying. Dylan felt an unwanted pang of guilt that he didn't want. She was still backed into a corner, shaking. Dylan walked close to her.

She screamed. Dylan felt the unwanted tears prickle his throat.

"M-mother," he whispered.

Chapter three. When a funeral happens.

Dylan was sitting in a church. He bounced his leg, thinking about what he was going to say about Von when it was his turn to speak. He shook his hands back and forth. His parents sat two rows away from him. He curled into his own little ball. No one wanted to sit near him. It was as if he has a horrible plague, like the illness that took over the first people of Richvill. But His parents still wanted him around for one more week, so that's why he was in a flowery, red-carpet church which had black curtains hanging from everything. He was wearing a black suit with a red clip-on tie. He pressed his back against the back of the chair. He looked around. His black eyes moved sadly, resting on everyone for a second or more.

He looked at Von's mother and father for a

second focusing on Von's mother's black hair that was braided into a bun.

She had her hand to her eyes, crying. She was dressed in a long black gown, low cut on the chest. It confused Dylan why someone would wear a dress like that at a funeral.

That's when an old woman sat down next to Dylan.

"Hello, dearie," she said.

"Hello, ma'am," he replied, shaking. He looked away from everyone.

"Why are you sitting here all alone?" she asked, touching his arm

"My parents are busy," he replied, sighing as he heard the first note on the piano, the slow and somber song of death. Dylan didn't know the name of the song, but it was played at funerals. He let his head bow to the ground. The music shook the church and vibrated amongst the walls. Each note did this. Dylan let out a soft cry.

"Damn it," he whispered underneath the music, as more tears fell down his cheeks. He closed his eyes, his whole body shaking, when suddenly, he felt a hand on his shoulder he looked up. It was Rachel. She was wearing a short black dress that hardly covered below the knee and a red glittery belt. She seemed to be staring at him, but he didn't say anything, so she just sat down next to him. She rubbed a circle into his back.

"It'll get easier," she choked out. Warm tears fell down her face.

Dylan let her hold his hand. She squeezed him.

"Maxton'll be here any minute," she mumbled, before she stopped talking, as a priest stood up from behind the organ. He stood in-front of a podium.

"We are gathered here today to say farewell to Veronica Arabia and to commit her into mourning, as she is in the hands of god," the priest began. Dylan felt his level of discomfort rise. He awkwardly moved in his seat.

"In the name of the Father, Son, and Holy Ghost, let her soul Rest in Peace. Now, may we have some friends and family say a final goodbye," the Priest explained.

Von's mother went up first.

"On April 4th, 6:30pm, my beautiful daughter Veronica was born. She grew up such a happy child, but during the whole of her growing up, she insisted on us calling her Von and cutting her hair. But she shouldn't have pretended to be a boy. She was such a beautiful woman, but God called her home early," his mother said, crying.

His dad didn't say anything, so it was Rachel's turn to speak. She navigated her way onto the platform. She had her hands on her sides.

"Von was a good friend. He always smiled. He helped us through some of our hardest days. He was a lantern in the darkest of times. I hope all the pain has stopped," Rachel said. She used her cane to get back to her seat. Then, it was Dylan's turn. He felt like he was struck with a hammer.

He walked down the red carpet up to the standing podium. He stood with his back straight and scanned the room. His thoughts disappeared as his mouth started moving.

"Two weeks ago, Von committed suicide. He wasn't doing it for attention," Dylan said, while he glanced at his parents and Von's, before counting.

"He just wanted an escape form the pain. He was in horrible amounts of pain. He just wanted the pain to stop, to stop when he looked in the mirror, to be accepted among the town, to be loved, to keep everyone happy. He was one of the bravest boys I've ever known. He just wanted to feel accepted!

"Why don't we accept him?!" Dylan said. Tears slowly started trailing down both of his cheeks, and his shoulders shook violently. He felt dizzy and started sobbing. That's when he ran off. He hated that he couldn't figure out how to handle his emotions when they stirred up like this, so he always ran. He ran out of the church into the parking lot.

"Stupid!" he screamed aloud, pointing to himself,

"Stupid! Stupid, stupid!" he screamed, falling down onto his knees. The concrete pulled his skin on the knees, as a rock cut him.

"I'm such an idiot! Why did I say that?!" he questioned, hitting himself in the head.

"You're so selfish..." he whispered, looking down at the ground. His tears made the concrete look like it freshly started raining, but only around him.

"God, why am I such an idiot?!" He felt as if his chest had been cut open his and his heart torn out.

Same with his organ, like someone was standing on him. He stayed on all fours, sobbing so hard, he was screaming. His voice echoed. He felt more tears fall down his cheeks.

He let out a harsh and loud screech. He sobbed. That's when he saw a blue convertible hood up. It was Maxton's car. Suddenly, the car stopped in front of him.

"Dylan? Are you hurt? Who hurt you?!" Maxton cried out, jumping out of the car and hugging Dylan.

"I'm sorry," Dylan whispered.

"Oh, it's the funeral, isn't it?" he whispered, pushing Dylan away to look into his eyes. Dylan nodded, shaking. The two boys embraced again, both crying.

If they could physically feel how calming the other was to them, they would probably have fallen over.

"I'm here," Maxton whispered before letting go of Dylan and helping him up.

"Let's get in there. I'm so sorry for being late," Maxton replied. Dylan was glad the whole town knew. Dylan couldn't handle his own emotions very well and didn't mean to make a scene. He was just sad. And shaken up. He pulled himself upwards as they went back into the church. The main service had ended, and everyone was loaded into the car to go to the graveyard.

"Dylan can ride with us," Maxton's mom told Dylan's mom.

Dylan looked at Maxton's mom. She was a tall skinny woman. Her curly hair was straightened and fell down to her back. Her hands were soft, and she had red lipstick on. Dylan let his hand fall on the fabricated car seat.

He was emotionally numb again. His eyes seemed to grow hollow. He just seemed to be gone.

"Dylan, are you okay?" Maxton's sing-songy voice grabbed onto him, making Dylan smile.

"Fine, I'm okay," he mumbled. The numbness returning, he stared at Maxton's eyes. Both of the two boys felt their hearts flutter, but romance didn't matter.

Dylan turned his head to the side, looking out the windows. Trees started blurring together as they passed by McDonald's and Walmart. They were there at the graveyard with about 90 graves. 80 of them were unmarked. About 10 had silver stones, and a total of 5 flowers on each of them were the limit.

Von's casket had been lowered into the ground. Dylan and his family stood around the hole. The family and friends cried around the hole #1 in the ground where the purple glittery coffin sat. Dylan and his family stood around the hole #I. The family and friends cried around the hole as the purple glitter coffin was lowered into the ground. The priest slightly pushed Dylan and Maxton apart slightly, before setting 3 handfuls of dirt onto the coffin. Dylan stared at the hole. He didn't feel anything, not sadness, not anger. A strange feeling like a pit in his stomach, slowly sinking down, was ripping him apart.

As he looked down at his hands and back to the grave, he thought, *If I died right here right now, would anyone except Maxton and Rachel come to my funeral? Would my parents even care?"*

Dylan tried to push these thoughts back, so it would feel like candlelight in a dream, but these horrible thoughts resurfaced after being pushed back like a cannon.

He stood there staring at the coffin.

Dylan felt a hand on his hands, He instinctively pulled away. He felt his shoulders shaking. He quickly got his emotions under control.

"Dylan, we should head home," he heard his mother say. She was standing a whole yard away from him.

"Yes, ma'am," he replied, feeling his shoulders fall to his side.

He took a few steps towards his mother, but his father gave him a stern look angry with black eyes, that said, "Step any closer to her, and you will be in a shallow grave yourself."

Dylan bit his lip hard. Dylan regretted everything. Why didn't he just pay up? Why was he so naive to assume that wasn't the only way pictures could be spread? He looked up and walked towards his car, the blue and red car that reflected the light, He put a hand over his eyes.

You're probably wondering why he covered his eyes. It was partially because the light hurt his eyes, and he felt tears threatening to spill over, (Could you blame him for warning to cry? He was at his best friend's funeral, and his own family was shunning him.) He felt a deep chill in his bones.

He reached for the door, pulling it open and staring at the black leather. He sat down, hardly noticing how cold it was.

"You're making a disgrace of the family, Dylan," his father started. Dylan sighed.

"I know, sir," he mumbled.

"You're ruining the Burr family blood line," his father continued.

"We're not in the 1700s anymore," Dylan whispered under his breath.

"What did you say?" his mother asked. She seemed really calm, just wondering what Dylan said.

"Nothing!" he replied, his breath suddenly accelerating.

"Okay, then," his mother said.

"Can we go home now?" Dylan asked, as they

drove around the one street town and turned around, repeating this process about 5 times. Dylan was annoyed.

"We're going somewhere, and Dylan, don't you say a word. Even if you did, you'd be ignored, understood?" his father hissed out.

Dylan hit his hand against his head a few times before saying, "Understood."

Dylan never thought he would think this, but god, did he wish he was at school. He'd be able to be left alone for a while, get a break from his dad.

Dylan laid his head against the car window as wheat and trees blurred together as he made another mental note. Funerals are exhausting and depressing. If those words were combined, what would they be? *Exhaustedepressing*? He found the word, *Exhaustapress*! He sounded like a psychopath. When Dylan woke up, the world was blurry.

He was still in the car and let out a sigh.

"Don't give me attitude!" his father snapped. Dylan had to stifle a laugh, because literally five minutes ago, he had said Dylan would be ignored. Dylan closed his eyes.

Chapter four. When you have to do a truth serum assignment and get locked in the car.

When Dylan opened his eyes, he was in the car. The black leather was now warm. He looked around for a split second, before saying, "Mother... Father?"

Then, he realized they were inside. He put his hand under the silver door handle and pulled it open. He let his feet hit the pavement and knocked on the door, He waited a few minutes before knocking again. He slid down against the door.

He waited for a while, before deciding to get in the car again. It was warmer in there than outside.

He was angry. He wanted to go inside but

knew his parents wouldn't open the door. If he broke into his own house, he'd be killed by an iron spike being inserted in his brain and another one into his spine. He shuddered at that thought. Dylan sat under the seats, so if anyone walked by, they couldn't see him. He felt sleep pull on his mind before he closed his eyes.

Dylan had an uneasy night. The thought of the car being broken into made him paranoid. Finally, he drifted off again. This process went on for 5 hours, so when the sun came up, Dylan just decided to head to school. His limbs felt tight. His neck popped with each turn. His knees hurt—scratch that—everything hurt. He headed across the street and pushed the fence open.

"Hey, Maxton, ya there?" he called out. The brown-haired boy searched the area, for him.

"Dylan, over here!" he said, behind the school. Dylan laughed. It was way too early to be there. School didn't start for another two hours, and any normal person would be asleep. Well, neither Dylan nor Maxton were normal.

By society's terms or their personalities, no, they weren't "weird." They were "limited edition." Dylan ran over to Maxton behind the school. When Dylan was there, Maxton pulled him close.

"You're gonna us killed," Dylan stated, blankly annoyed.

"Shh, no one's around," Maxton replied, just hand-sliding over Dylan's back in a circular motion.

"True, but still, everyone's already on my ass. I don't want them on your ass, too," Dylan replied, leaning into Maxton's touch.

"I'm 100% percent sure my parents know. They just don't want to do anything, about it," Maxton replied.

"Lucky." Dylan replied. His voice was dry but

still had its own warmth. "My parents are treating me like an animal," he added, biting the inside of his mouth.

"What did they do?" Maxton asked.

"Ya know, won't let me sit near them, talk to them, locked me outside the house in the car. I think they'd be happier if I was gone," Dylan said so bluntly, it shocked Maxton.

"That's not true," Maxton replied, worried, wrapping his arms protectively around Dylan in a hug.

"Yes, it is, and you know I'm not lying," he said, feeling a tinge of guilt pulling on his eyes, almost causing the burning, salty liquid of tears to come out.

"Your parents are massive di- jerks," Maxton caught himself before he finished that statement.

"My father is. Mother isn't. She's just so brainwashed by the guy, she's too scared to leave him," he explained.

"What about Kathrine, your sister?" Maxton asked.

"She's not my sister," he replied.

"Dylan, don't be like that," Maxton said, shocked by the anger that was quivering in pure rage.

"I'm not calling my father's affair, 'my sister.' He hit my mom so hard that day for telling him off. She had very single right to!" Dylan exclaimed, throwing his hands in an exasperated motion.

"But you do love her, don't you?" Maxton asked. Sweat was slowly dripping down his cheek, hitting his neck.

"Yeah, I mean, I guess I have to," he said. Dylan knew he was lying. He loved Kathrine. He just was angry and spraying words he didn't mean and didn't care what they could have meant.

The two boys sat behind the school until

Maxton said, "Do you think they'll brain- spike us?"

Dylan's eyes widened. God, did he hate that term "brain-spiked," when someone takes a full or sharp metal rod and slowly screws it into your brain. After that happens, your spine shatters.

"I don't know, Maxton. I really don't know," he said, touching Dylan's hand.

Maxton finally let how strong he was just fade away.

"I hate this town. Idiot teachers, idiot teenagers—why is everyone here so stupid? Except you or Rachel, of course."

"Maxton! Someone could have heard you by now," he said, laughing. Dylan hated that, when he was annoyed, he laughed at the person.

"It's still 6:05. Kids don't get even near the school till 7:12, so use this hour and six minutes, to say what we want to say."

"All right, then." Dylan said, smirking, biting his lower lip again.

Maxton smiled at Dylan, his warm eyes before looking around and giving Dylan a kiss on the lips. His heart pounded.

Dylan wanted to pull away. They were being stupid. Couldn't they be stupid teenagers, just this once? Yes and no.

Yes, because no one was around. No one would see them. The whole town was asleep.

No, because they were both boys.

Dylan held onto Maxton's shoulders, so he wouldn't fall against the brick wall of the school. He kissed back. Maxton's hands were warm. They stayed in this position for about 2-3 minutes, before Maxton moved away.

"I wish we could do that in public. Like, I don't know, go up to someone and kiss, then run away, and no one could do a damn thing," he whispered.

"Me, too. I mean, in the 2000s, we could do that," Dylan said, pushing himself back into the brick wall.

"2100's SUCK!" Maxton yelled. Dylan choked on laughter.

"Oh my, no, Maxton," he responded before erupting into a convulsive fit of laughter. His eyes started watering, as even his cheeks started hurting.

"I'm sorry. I couldn't help it," he whispered.

"No, I'm not mad. Just, that was funny," he replied, wiping his eyes.

Before the two boys knew it, an hour had turned five, five minutes and five minutes turned into none, as the first kid came out of his car and started studying.

"Wow, that went by fast," Dylan commented, as they left from behind the school. Well, Maxton waited several minutes, to make it look less suspicious.

They both walked around and talked the whole time until everyone in the courtyard was called into the one-story, blue and white school. Dylan and Maxton had first hour with Mr. Bird. The thing with Mr. Bird was, he was a lot nicer than every other teacher, but little did they know what his experiment for today would be.

"The Effects of Truth Serum" would ruin two of his students' lives.

When Dylan and Maxton walked into the class, Mr. Bird was sitting, cleaning up his glasses. He had brown hair that parted at the side and a crooked tooth. He wore a black sweatshirt and blue khaki pants.

"Hello, Max and Dylan," he greeted the two boys.

Maxton returned the "hello." Dylan just waved. He was awkward.

Mr. Bird stood in front of the whole class and pointed at the board.

"Okay, class, today we're learning about Truth Serum. We will be doing a lab," the teacher explained, before reaching into his cabinet and pulling out about 13 medicine cups and a gallon of a red liquid that shook every time he moved it.

"All right. So, for this experiment you will have to drink this truth serum, and then you go outside, and a group of three will ask you a question and document your answers," he explained.

Dylan waited for his cup to be filled exactly halfway, before taking a tiny swig, swishing it in his mouth back and forth before trying to figure out how he could get the hell out of this situation. He swallowed the tiny bit, which made his tongue feel weird, tingly and numb. Dylan made a face as the bitterness of the serum took over his taste buds. Finally, he took another sip, this one larger, knocking back most of it to the point, there were too little drops left. Suddenly, his whole face went numb as the classroom around him started glowing. The next thing he knew, he was floating, looking down at the classroom, but still in control of his own body.

"Dylan, are you okay?" he heard Maxton ask. His voice was distorted but still clear, like an old phonograph.

"Yeah, I think. Am I tripping?" Dylan asked.

He heard the teacher laugh.

"No, Dylan, it's just the side effects," the teacher explained.

"Dylan?" Rachel laid her soft hand on Dylan's shoulder. Her blonde, curled hair was in a braid. She was wearing the same outfit from the funeral.

"Yeah?" Dylan replied.

"Answer my question. When's your birthday?" she asked.

"1/25," he replied.

"Okay, when's your birthday?" Dylan asked Rachel.

"9/15," Rachel replied.

Suddenly, one kid, Markus, who everyone hated, stepped up. He was muscular and in football, had blonde hair, and he had a shirt on that said, "I'd be paid to shut up."

He looked at Dylan, smirking, then asked this, "Okay, so, umm, are you gay?"

Dylan felt his heart pounding. He held a finger over his mouth for a few seconds, before saying, "Does it matter?" Dylan felt emotionally exhausted again. He hated this so much.

"Well, duh, you know God hates gays," Markus said.

Dylan had to fight with every ounce of willpower in his body. He tried to speak, but his throat was dry.

"Oh, so you are," Markus said, smirking.

"Why are we trusting anything the other says, when Truth Serum causes false memories?" Rachel quickly said this, saving the situation.

Markus seemed annoyed and went off, asking someone else questions. The teacher glared at Rachel but didn't say anything.

Dylan fell silent for a few minutes. He just wanted to be out of this class. He hated the fact that he was still floating.

"Hey, Rachel, how did you know where I was at the funeral, yesterday?" Dylan asked, looking over the curly-haired girl.

"I recognized your voice when you whispered 'damn,'" she replied, smiling at Dylan. She was caring, accepting, supportive, and beautiful. If Dylan were interested in girls, they would be a thing. Rachel Piper was short and frail. Her eyes were blue, not the milky white, people would assume she would have, as a blind person. Her nose was quite small.

She had a passion for reading, via Braille or audiobook. She was extremely kind.

"Thanks for comforting me," Dylan thanked Rachel, smiling.

"You're welcome," she replied, holding her pink cane in her left hand. She was allowed to leave class five minutes early.

Dylan wanted to sleep, at that point. The Truth Serum had made him feel dizzy, sick to his stomach, and now he just wanted to sleep the effects of the serum off. He laid his head down on the hard wood desk table before he felt a warm hand on his arm.

"What the-"he began, before he realized it was just Maxton.

"Hey, sorry for scaring you. I just wanted to ask if you were okay. You seemed drained."

Dylan, felt words bubbling to his mouth, words that could get him killed, so he swallowed them. The words burned his throat.

"You're - I mean, yeah," he replied. Dylan mentally told himself off for that slip up. He wished he could let these words loose like a balloon, but he couldn't. He felt heat all over his face and on the back of his neck, on his ears, cheeks, under his eyes.

"Why do I blush like this?!" he questioned.

"Ohh, Dylan's gay!" he heard someone yell from behind him. Another kid joined in, and Dylan still wanted to sleep. His eyes burnt. It was going to be a long day, and with that thought, Dylan's fate was sealed.

The class ended, so he and Rachel went to go to, the next class, when Markus grabbed Dylan's hair. Dylan screamed, but Markus didn't stop until a teacher told him to do so. That was the first injury of the day. Dylan went to his next class. The one after that was nothing that important.

But hell broke loose at lunch. Dylan felt the

tension in the cafeteria. The air was hard to breathe. Each breath took more effort than the last. He went into line, grabbed a slice of the weird golden-brown bread with tomato that had been smushed up, and spread out on to bread with frozen cheese sprinkled on top. That was what everyone in Richvill called pizza.

Dylan walked over to Rachel, flopping down, causing the chair to whine and complain about the weight of the two teens.

"Hi, Dylan," Rachel replied, hearing him.

"Hey, Rach," he replied, touching her hand. Dylan never noticed how soft her hands were, but he didn't mind. It was rare finding someone with soft hands in Richvill, since the chemicals in soap were so harsh.

"How are you doing?" Rachel asked, moving her hand away from Dylan's, setting it on her mostly frozen milk She grabbed it and shook it near her ear, searching for the sound of liquid, but no sound was heard, just a hunk moving up and down.

"How do you freeze milk?!" Rachel exclaimed, setting the carton back on her tray, before moving onto the peanut butter and jelly sandwich.

"I thought milk couldn't freeze since they injected that fish gene into it back in 2110?" Dylan asked.

"Holy shit! Ew," she muttered, setting the carton back onto her tray, then setting the carton in the trash can.

"I'm not a big milk drinker anyway," she added. Dylan inhaled sharply before laughing until he couldn't help it. After a few minutes, Dylan seemed to snap into reality and stopped laughing as a red tint painted his face until he looked around.

"Where's Max?" he asked.

"I think he went to the library," Rachel said,

resting her hand on her cheek, finishing her sandwich.

"Oh okay. Hey, I'm gonna go to the bathroom. If I'm not back before lunch is over, I'll just meet you in class," Dylan said, pushing himself up like a spring walking towards the stop sign that was the pass. He moved his hands away from themselves like he was spreading out dominoes. He stared down at the keyboard that floated circling his waist. He moved his fingers upwards, before filling out the hall pass.

"How long will your visit to the bathroom take?"

Dylan sighed and put, "about 10 minutes." It was a freaking bathroom break. Why did he even need to fill that in?! He headed towards the bathroom, did his business, and was washing his hands. He pumped two pumps of soap and let the cold water rinse them. He heard the stall door open. His joints and muscles froze up from the startle. It was that golden-haired boy.

"I knew I smelled trash in here!" he said. walking towards Dylan.

"It's a bathroom. Of course, it smells, or maybe you're smelling yourself," Dylan stated simply. He had to wash his hands another time, or else the thought would annoy him for the rest of the day, so he got the next two pumps of soap, rubbing his hands together, rinsing soap over it.

Suddenly, he felt another hand on his shoulder that yanked him backwards. He hit the hard, ceramic floor.

Dylan's ankle exploded in pain.

He let out a pained moan, pulling his legs into his chest. The golden-haired boy kicked Dylan in the shin and the side, knocking him over. He punched Dylan in the chest and face. Dylan wasn't able to dodge.

He couldn't move. He felt his back being

kicked and punched. He tried to move to fight back and to breathe. He felt a cold blade hit the back of his neck, He felt a warm liquid slowly drip down his neck.

"You should be spiked, faggot! Why don't they spike you?" the brown-haired boy said, pressing down slowly into his neck.

Dylan screamed as he felt the knife cut muscle.

"Stop screaming!" The golden-haired boy yelled, slamming a hand against Dylan's mouth. Dylan bit hard on the golden-haired boy's hand and tasted the iron-like taste of blood. His face contorted in disgust.

"What the hell?! You bit me!" The golden-haired boy screamed, yanking away, shaking his bleeding hand.

"You cut my neck!" Dylan shouted in response, slapping his hand over the gash, as blood splashed to the floor.

"I'm telling a teacher!" the golden-haired boy yelled, before running off. More blood dripped down from Dylan's neck to the floor. Stabbing pain covered his neck. The world was going in and out of focus.

He wasn't sure how much blood was dripping down, but there was a small puddle. He tried to move but got even dizzier. He felt himself wobble, like he was on an uneasy patch of ground. He felt himself zone in and out until he couldn't stand up anymore. He fell down to his knees, staring at the blood pool. More blood leaked out every time blood dripped down. Dylan heard a splash. He tried to count how many times he heard this splash but couldn't focus on anything.

He fell on his stomach, still breathing.

"Am I going to die?" That was the only thought going through his practically empty head. Death, at this point, this word seemed more of a theme than a conclusion. Death was both a theme and a conclusion: a theme in people's life and a conclusion to one's own story, but this was not how Dylan would die.

Suddenly, the boys' bathroom door flew open.

"Dylan Burr! Young man, come to my off-"the principal screamed but then got caught by the image of the brown-haired boy's eyes open, a hardly breathing child, with two thick lines of blood on his neck dripping down to the floor. His eye was swollen shut, and his lip was busted. The principal crouched down next to Dylan, putting a hand on the boy's back.

"Hey, Hey, Dylan. Can you hear me?" he asked.

Dylan nodded slightly, still going in and out of consciousness. The principal got his phone and dialed 911, He felt bad, because Dylan's family would have to pay for the ambulance trip out of town—about 15 minutes.

10-15 minutes later, Dylan was lifted up by two men, put on a stretcher, and was bombed with questions, but he couldn't keep up. He hardly felt the needle in his arm, nor did he see the blood being pumped into him. Time stopped for him. Nothing changed. He felt his eyes finally close, as he was met with the peaceful darkness of unconsciousness.

Rachel was the first visitor about two days later. Dylan had been unconscious for those two days he was on oxygen, but it still scared Rachel to death, hearing all these new sounds, smelling the scent of depression and death.

She talked to him for hours on end, telling him how to do the work at school, about what was happening beyond the hospital's prison-like walls.

Rachel stayed with him for two days. Dylan's family didn't even visit him once.

When Dylan woke up, he said, "I wish I died in the attack." He whispered this statement.

Society hating you gets to you after a while. After your family stops loving you, your mind goes into places where Dylan didn't want to talk, places were everything seemed dark and helpless.

He sat there in bed, his eyes glued to the familiar prison like walls.

When suddenly Maxton came to visit him, he looked Dylan over, seeming to take all of his injuries in at the same time, noticing the oxygen tube hanging from his nose the IV sticking out of his arm and the cords hanging off of his chest.

"I'm glad you're awake," Maxton told him, smiling, moving slowly to Dylan's bed.

Dylan smiled at Maxton. He seemed not to be able to find words. It had been like that since he woke up, unable to project the thoughts out of his mind, but he knew that would change soon.

"Rachel told me you're not gonna talk much," he said, sitting on the bed. The bed made a sound.

Dylan took a deep breath as his own weight

started getting too heavy for him.

"That's okay. I know you're probably mad at me for not coming to visit you. I only found out you were in the hospital yesterday, and it was like midnight. I didn't want to bother you at that time," he explained. Dylan smiled. He was a little mad at first, but he didn't care now. Now that Maxton was there, it was cheesy. He knew that but did he care how cheesy it was? It was the truth.

"Maxton, I'm scared." He took a deep breath, before looking at Maxton as he whispered this.

"I know, Dylan," he replied, taking Dylan's hand and squeezing it. Maxton looked back up from his hand.

"They know," he said, his body erupting in shakes and trembles.

"I know, Dylan."

"My family's going to do conversion therapy."

Dylan let that sentence settle in the room. Maxton's eyes filled over with tears.

"Don't blame yourself. Hell, we knew this was a risk," Dylan whispered back.

"I know, but I told you I would protect you," Maxton finally said. Dylan had forgotten that day in the woods.

How did it go again? Oh yes.

It was raining that night. Even the clouds could feel the emotions in the air. Dylan had run out of his house to cool down. He couldn't remember exactly why he was so rattled up, probably after he found out about his father's affair. He went to go cool down. He had tripped while walking and rolled down a muddy area. When he stopped rolling, he hit a tree, and that hurt. When Maxton heard Dylan's fall, he went to go check on him.

"Are you okay?" He had asked, reaching a large hand down to help him up.

"Yeah." Dylan had replied. His cheek was bleeding, and his clothing was stained.

"I'll give you my shirt," Maxton replied.

"Thanks."

Dylan quickly changed, holding the muddied shirt in his arms against his chest, like a puppy. The air had no tension, as though no bad thing had happened. It was as if the stars had finally aligned.

"Hey, are you ok?" That question stood out to Dylan the most, so he told Maxton the truth. He had a lot on his mind, so he just told Maxton everything, about the affair, about the arguments, about the death threats written on his locker.

Maxton wrapped his arms around Dylan and whispered this to him, "I'm going to protect you, no matter what."

Maxton was warm. Dylan was shaking as he slowly felt tears hit his cheeks.

"Hey, it's okay," Maxton whispered. Dylan wasn't sure if he was having a mental breakdown or was just upset. He didn't want to be like the people who dyed their hair, gave themselves bangs, and called those things mental breakdowns.

"Dylan, can I hold you?" Maxton asked. His arms were in this weird position, as if he was going to scoop Dylan up, Dylan nodded, and Maxton hugged him tightly, so tightly that every breath was hard, but, at the same time, peace washed over them. Neither one seemed to want to ruin this moment.

.... even though there were about 143 people who did.

Part two.

A few things go wrong and more about Rachel. What will happen to Dylan and Maxton?

Part two.

A few things go wrong and more about Rachel. What will happen to Dylan and Maxton?

Chapter five. So, are you prepared for a Rachel? takeover?

Rachel was sitting underneath a tree. The wind blew her blonde hair. She was taking in the sounds, allowing herself to relax. She knew Dylan was safe for now. She had known Dylan ever since they were little. It was hard imagining a world with him not in it. If her were spiked, would anyone even cry, except her? Or would his body join the many buried underneath Richvill's ground?

Rachel shook her head at that thought, her curly blonde hair bouncing around as she did this movement. She was born nearly blind. She had some vision left, only being able to see light, like if you had a funnel. She hated this. Rachel pushed herself upwards on her left arm and gracefully stood up. Her pink dress slightly blew back and forth, slapping her legs, but she didn't mind. She put her cane in front of herself, taking a step. After she slid the cane back and forth, she guided herself away from the tree, heading down the street. She was nervous. She hated going home. Her parents treated her like a baby, assisting her. They fed her and helped with basic self needs. Being treated like that drove her crazy and made her want to curl into a ball and die, but she didn't want to worry her parents.

While walking down the street, she heard cars zoom by. As she tried crossing the street, she almost got hit but made it to the other side. She waited to feel with her cane the hole in her walkway, so she could know which house was hers. When her cane went into that little hole, she moved forward to her two-story house with brown bricks and a grey roof.

She felt for her keys that were in her dress' belt band. She unclipped them, then slowly inserted the key into the keyhole, twisting it, then pulling it open. Warm air slightly pushed her hair back as she stood in the doorway.

"Mom! Dad! I'm home!" she called out, hanging her cane, then walking to her room. In her own house, she didn't need her cane. She knew where everything was.

"Hi, honey." her father, whose hair had turned grey, answered her. He had on a blue shirt and black jeans. He spoke slowly, as if talking to a child.

Rachel repeated that tone and just said, "Hello."

Rachel could feel her father roll his eyes. The air was slightly thick, so Rachel went to her room and sat on her bed. She curled in on herself. No, she didn't cry. She had only cried once in the past 3 years. Never mind, scratch that. She cried when she read Von's letter.

The point was, Rachel wasn't a cryer, but when she did cry, it was really hard to calm her down, and Rachel hated how vulnerable it made her feel.

Rachel lay on her side curled in a ball, shivering. At the same time, she didn't have enough willpower to move or fight against the unwanted wave of exhaustion she was fighting. Like a dam, after a while, the material would run down, and water would slowly leak in until finally there was a break. As sleep washed over Rachel, leaving her defenseless, wind was blowing her hair. When her senses returned, the sea pulled on her nose. As water droplets entered each breath, she pushed herself on her hand.

"Mom! Dad?" she called out. No response. Was her brother playing a prank on her? He would do that, take her blindness into his advantage, and set things up in her room. Or, was she dreaming? Rachel wasn't sure. She walked around the area, feeling something squishy beneath her feet. She moved her toes back and forth. Sand! She recognized this texture.

Who wouldn't!

Now, time to pin down where she was. She was obviously not in Richvill, and even if she was, it wouldn't be Richvill. It would be maybe what lay beyond what Richvill taught her about. She felt the air push on her, moving her arms back and forth. Nothing was in front of he, so she proceeded forward, continuing her path, her feet slowly sinking into the sand. Words were popping up in her head, but she wasn't sure of the meaning.

She knew the word she was looking for started with a "B." What was it?

"Bi-" Rachel started, but then realized that wasn't the word she was looking for—beach! She smiled. Finally, the word came to mind. She was happy as her foot hit something hard, sending a small amount of pain up her leg like a ping pong ball. She sat down, rubbing a hand over her bleeding foot.

"What was that?" she thought to herself,

before running her hand through the sand, slipping her hand over the hard surface she hit had her foot against. She lifted it up and set it in her lap. She felt its warmth. It seemed to weave its way around her fingers. She felt a hole and put her hand in it. Hollows. Shell up to her ear, slowly listening, as waves crashed back and forth. She let her mind run away from her. She took that beautiful sound and the adjustment of the light, as darkness slowly was swallowing her. It was like being in a tunnel.

"The sun's going down," she whispered to herself/ That's when she felt a warm hand on her shoulders.

"Rachel, sweetie, it's time to wake up." It was her father, but she shook her head, and suddenly, she was back in her room. Her body was slightly twisted in her covers, and her blanket felt oddly warm.

"It's dinner," her father informed her, looking down at the girl in the blankets.

"Okay, Dad," she replied, pushing herself up, slowly pulling the blankets off from around her waist, and, getting up, she felt two strong hands grab her shoulders, gently guiding her to the table, Rachel didn't mind this that much. Chairs were hard. Sometimes, she could miss them.

"All right. I made soup. Ready?" She sighed. She hated mealtime. She could easily feed herself. It was just that they wouldn't let her. Even if she tried, they would explain that she was blind and would burn herself, if they let eat for herself.

They even did this in public. That was why Rachel was always at Dylan's house. His family let her eat by herself, and Rachel loved that feeling of freedom. It's the little things we always need to advantage of.

Rachel tried to feel for her soup but felt a warm metal spoon put to her lips. She let him feed her for about ten seconds until she finally snapped.

"I'm not stupid! Stop treating me like I am!" she screamed, slamming her hands against the table.

"Sweetie, you're not stupid. Now, let's finish your soup," Her father continued trying to get her to take a sip.

"I can feed myself!" she yelled. Anger bubbled up inside her, boiling over. She felt her cheeks grow hot from rage.

Her father ignored this, so Rachel reached forward and felt the warm ceramic bowl, pulling it to herself, spoon in hand, and put the soup to her mouth, eating by herself.

"See?!" She asked, annoyed. The rage hadn't worn off, so she was on edge, still.

"Rachel, I'm sorry. I just thought since you couldn't see…" her father began. Rachel cut him off.

"that I was an infant and needed your help with everything?" She questioned, her elbow wrapped around her soup. The glossy ceramic made her arm slide.

"No, I thought you would hurt yourself!"

Rachel wasn't hungry anymore. She stood up and went to her room, rubbing her hands along the long soft fabric of her nightgown. She pulled it off, falling on her butt.

She rubbed the fabric against her face pulling the fabric over her head. She fell asleep again. This time, no weird dreams that made her not be able to tell where she was, but no dreams at all.

Her dad woke her up. It was Saturday, so Rachel went to go see Dylan. She was guided to his house and knocked on the door. She heard feet shuffle. Then, an angry hand yanked her in by the shoulder.

"What did you know about this?!" Dylan's father screamed at her, spit spraying all over /her face.

"Know about what?!" Rachel asked, confused Why was he mad at her. Where was Dylan?

"That my son was a faggot!" he screamed at her.

"Don't call him that," Rachel whispered, using a voice she reserved only for assholes, and this asshole was a good reason for that voice.

"I'm sorry, but are you actually tellin' me what to do?" Dylan's father moved his neck, as if examining her. Rachel heard his neck pop.

"Yes. Yes, I am. I don't understand what gives you the right to be such a piece of trash, maybe scum of the earth if you're lucky." she said, smiling creepily.

"How long did you know Dylan was gay?!" he asked her again. Rachel turned her head away from Dylan's screaming father.

"I don't know," she replied with a simple shrug of the shoulders. In reality, her mind and heart were racing, her heart doing somersaults in her chest over and over again.

"Lies," Dylan's father said.

"Where's Dylan?" Rachel asked, moving her hand across the empty air in front her.

"Not important. You know what? Answer my question, and I'll answer yours." His father hesitated.

So, Rachel used 1–3-word sentences to answer each question. The conversation went a bit like this.

"How long did you know about their relationship?"

"I didn't."

"When did he come out to you?

"He didn't."

90% of the conversation went like that. Dylan's father asked a question, and Rachel replied that she didn't know a thing. She was lying about not knowing anything. After he grilled her, it was Rachel's turn.

"Where's Dylan?" she asked, slamming her hands against her lap.

"Conversion therapy."

Rachel felt her breath die in her throat.

"You did what?!" she asked, rage pushing, onto her voice like a knife through bread.

Rachel threw her hands in the air in an angered motion.

"It's good for his health!" His father tried to reason with Rachel. That just made her even angrier.

"No, it's not! I know what those places do! I've talked to kids who went through shit like that! It's brainwashing! It's bullshit! Just like this town, it's all bullshit!" Rachel proclaimed, as she felt as if a weight was lifted from her shoulders. Silence flooded the room as Rachel slapped a hand over her mouth.

"What did I just say?" she thought to herself.

"It'll cure him, even if it kills him. Maybe a spike to the brain would fix him." Rachel tensed up at that part. She wanted to kill him, right there and then. She wasn't thinking, though as she had this thought in her mind.

"Something needs to change, and it starts with me." She felt her body relax. She didn't want to be there at all, not even a tiny bit.

Dylan's father made her go home. As she was walking home, she wasn't sure how she would change anything, but she knew she would have an idea, and all she needed was an air computer offline, a printer, and a bunch of earmuffs.

Rachel ran into her room, leaving her cane on the floor in her rush. She slammed the door shut.

Chapter six. Rachel is a badass revolutionary.

Rachel moved her hands apart as a keyboard circled her. She moved both of their hands over her ears. As she felt a slight weight on her small ears, she started rapping, hearing every letter she was clicking on.

"Fight against Flormorent and change the world. We will not be spiked."

That was the beginning of about 45 posters. She stayed up all night and didn't even care about her mandatory church visit. It all seemed a thing of the past. She stood there, moving in circles, to make sure she hit every single folder. Her fingers hurt from typing so rapidly for who knows how long. She traced her finger in a circular motion but then abruptly stopped.

"Are you sure you'd like to print out 45

posters on the PFP?" the computer called out. Rachel bit down hard on her lip. This was it. If she printed these posters, she could start a revolution.

Was she ready for this responsibility?

Yes, she had been born ready for about five years now. She was done putting up with this.

"Yes, print 34, now," she said, her heart slightly pounding, as she felt paper slowly appear in her hands. The slightly warm sheet had braille on it. She traced her finger across it, smiling when it matched what she wrote.

Now, she needed to figure out where to put them. The first thought was the church, so she grabbed her Bible and put the pages into it. She shook her leg up and down.

"Rachel, honey, what's wrong?" Rachel's mother asked. Her hair was in a ponytail, and she started combing Rachel's hair back. Rachel tried walking forward.

"Nothing, Mom," Rachel replied, pushing her posters back deeper into the Bible.

When she brought them into church, she waited until services were over, and while the adults were talking, she snuck outside. Using her cane to navigate to the front sign, she stuck one poster into the lines of the sign. She repeated this process until the sign was covered, and then she snuck back in. She knew her church like the back of her mind, so it wasn't such a big deal.

"Oh, hey, Ray!" She heard a voice call out from behind her. It was Maxton! She would recognize his voice anywhere.

"Hi, Maxton," Rachel said, turning around, holding her hand out, hoping he was behind her.

She felt a cold hand slip into hers He squeezed both of her hands, before slipping away from her grip. They had no romantic feelings for each other. Maxton saw Rachel as his little sister.

"You look great," he complimented, tapping her head, Rachel smiled in spite of herself.

"Thanks," Rachel replied. She felt her head fall forward. She was tired.

"Are you okay?" Maxton asked.

"Tired, very tired," she said simply.

"I get it. I am, too," Maxton responded, shrugging his shoulders.

"Can I show you something?" Rachel asked, her tone hardening. She took a few deep breaths, waiting for his response.

"Sure," Maxton said hesitantly, as if waiting for something to hurt him.

Rachel grabbed his arm, guiding him to the sign.

She heard Maxton draw out a gasp.

"You... did all this in one night? No wonder

you're exhausted," he whispered. Suddenly, Rachel heard footsteps. That's when Rachel got an idea. She whispered an apology to Maxton and then kissed him on the lips. She heard him let out a muffled, startled sound.

"Just go along with it," she squeezed his shirt, as she felt her heart pound. She didn't love him, not like this. She wanted to pull away, but she stayed until she heard this. It was the pastor.

"Oh, that's where you two sinners went," he said, lovingly laughing, slightly. Rachel pushed herself away from Maxton.

"Yes, sir," she replied, feeling her cheeks grow red. She was blushing, of course. This always happened.

"I'll leave you to it. Just remember, if you do anything unholy, I will always forgive your sins," he explained before just walking away.

Rachel waited until she heard a door shut.

"What the hell?!" Maxton snapped, turning on his foot.

"I'm sorry. I thought that it would be suspicious if anyone saw us together and then saw the posters. They would kill you! So, I made out with you, hoping that they would think we were together and not think about the posters!" Rachel replied. slamming her foot against the hard ground

Maxton sighed and stated, still angry, "Just screw it! Where's Dylan?" he asked, moving a hand through his hair.

"Therapy, conversion therapy," Rachel responded sadly, as she remembered why she hated this town so much, out of about 100,000 reasons why she hated this hell hole.

Maxton let out a growl under his breath before glaring up at Rachel.

"You don't tell me until now?!" he questioned.

"You didn't ask," she replied, tensing up. Her

brother yelled at her a lot, but when you yell at the wrong person for the right amount of time, you get a bullet through the head. Rachel always forgot he was dead.

"You should have told me! I thought he was running late!"

"It doesn't matter! Okay?! You know, now." Rachel yelled, even more annoyed that she was wrong. What was happening to Dylan did matter.

An awkward, tense silence filled the air as Rachel pulled on her dress, regretting everything she'd said. She heard Maxton walk away as a small void of loneliness pulled onto her. She gripped her shoulders, allowing her fingernails to sink into her them. She stayed in this position for about maybe 15 seconds; then, she released the painful grip on herself.

"Damnit," she mumbled. Her body shook as she used her cane, slowly taking a deep breath. Her hand was wrapped around the soft part as she tapped, instead of sliding. She went back into the church, as if she were on a mission. She took a few steps before realizing.

Shit, she didn't have anything to record with. Her plan was to record around the church. Why she wasn't sure on what she would catch, so she started making a plan. She put her Bible under one of the seats, the first one to the left. She felt the plush carpet and held her Bible under the seat before dropping it.

She heard her mother's footsteps approaching.

"Rachel, home, now," she said, not angry, just using short words.

"Okay," Rachel replied. They never checked if she had her Bible, so she could just casually say she left it, and her parents would let her go get it.

The walk home was about 6 minutes of silence, as if waiting for something to happen. Hurried footsteps and the vroom of cars filled all of her senses. Her heart slightly pounded against her chest. She heard a truck backing up and heard the back open. Cold air started whipping her. She took a few more hurried steps. The family of three walked into their home, as Rachel put on a fake startled face, moving her hands around, as if feeling for something.

"Mom! Dad! Could I go back to the church? I forgot my Bible," she stated. Her voice shook.

"For heaven's sake, go get it!" her mom replied. Rachel ran to her room. She sought a small bug that she could use with her computer to listen in on what happened when everyone was gone. Rachel felt a wave of guilt sneak up on her for doing this. Why should she?

The town was screwed up, and it was her responsibility to try and fix the town.

Rachel moved quickly, as she felt raindrops pound against her face. She blinked them out of her useless eyes. She continued walking as she smelled the sickly, sour scent of the church's candles. She knocked on the metal doors and heard the shuffle of feet.

"Oh, hello, Rachel. What's wrong?" Rachel heard the pastor ask.

"Uhh, yeah. I'm sorry, sir, but I forgot my Bible. Can I go get it?" she asked, tapping her foot against the concrete.

"Of course," he replied. Rachel felt silence. As her body went stiff, she forced herself to bend over and reached under the chair, setting the metal listening device under the seat. She felt the heavy leathery book and stood up.

She left and headed home and went into her room. Then, she sat on her bed, summoned a keyboard and headphones and took a deep breath. It was silent for about 5 minutes, except the sound of cleaning, some footsteps, and pages flipping.

She sighed, until she heard a voice. It was

Dylan's.

"I'm not mad at him! I'm mad at you!" His voice bounced around the empty church. Rachel covered her ears. A ringing sound made her tense up.

"Dylan, you do know that homosexuality is a sin," another voice said. Rachel wasn't sure who it was, which was strange, from how small the town was.

She heard Dylan scream and felt her body shake slightly. She hated this but still needed the information if she wanted to change anything. She needed to rebel from the outside and then move in, sort of like a predator circling the prey from the outside, getting closer and closer, and then, attacking it. The town ran off of brainwashing.

Maybe this could be a reality check, hearing children scream for unknown reasons. It would make any mother want to soothe the crying child or stop what was hurting them.

Rachel listened to screams and the whirl of electric shocks.

They could fry his mind, Rachel thought to herself. It was a thought she didn't want to think about; losing Dylan would destroy her. She wanted to stop, but she needed to know what happened if she could record this. It would help stop these practices.

"Dylan, I'm so sorry," she whispered as she felt warm tears slip down her cheeks into her dress. She tried to stop the unwanted stream, but it didn't work. She tried to inhale, but her tight throat forced tears down her cheeks. She needed to listen, but she couldn't.

"We're under the belief that homosexuality is an addiction and mental illness we're trying to cure. This is for your own good, Dylan." Rachel heard someone say, Dylan didn't respond--not that Rachel could hear that well. She heard mentions of trauma and making him remember it, Rachel had a feeling that the only trauma they would get was physical abuse, as hands of his angry father would slam against him.

"I'm going to show you a picture of a man," Rachel heard the voice say. Rachel curled into a ball, listening to this. Her heart pounded. She heard Dylan's voice—and then, his scream. Rachel squeezed herself as more tears fell down her cheeks. She realized something. Dylan was going to reach his snapping point soon, and that would be terrifying. It was scary to see people angry, but rage and pain were never a good combo.

"I don't think this is working," Dylan stayed. His voice was shaking. Was he crying? Rachel wanted to hug him, pull him away from that hell hole.

"Should we shock you some more?" she heard the voice reply. She felt her body go rigid.

"You've already shocked me enough. Go ahead," he mumbled the "go ahead" part.

More words Rachel couldn't understand, or maybe she did understand; she just refused to accept what she was hearing, blocking out her mind.

"It's bullshit!" she heard another boy scream.

Rachel had to stop listening. She took the earbuds off, sent the keyboard away, and then started crying. Her body erupted in sobs. She hated it here. She wanted to run away.

She grabbed the pillow on her bed and set a pillow over her face and screamed a scream full of rage and sadness. She heard someone talk towards her. She sat up and screamed, hurting. Her throat started aching every time she tried to scream again. She sat there until she felt like removing the pillow off her head.

Chapter seven. Losing your voice! And the first step of the rebellion.

Rachel stopped screaming, slowly moving her pillow out of her face. Her throat felt like a bullet was being torn through her raspy breath. Rage stopped wrapping around her like a vortex of ice.

She tried to speak, but all she emitted were pained words that no one could hear her.

Tears still ravaged her cheeks like a flood. Was Dylan going to be the same when conversation therapy was over?

Those were some of the 50 thousand things going through her mind.

One thought entered her mind: *Was Dylan going to die?*

Rachel shuddered at that thought. If he was going to die, how would he? Would he be shocked until his brain fried? Or would a spike go through his head? Rachel held herself, slowly rocking back and forth as more tears fell down onto her dress. She rocked back and forth, crying. She ended up sobbing. Her shoulders gently moved upward and downwards.

She tried to take a deep breath, but she hiccupped as this thought slammed against her mind like a flood.

This is all your fault. All of it is your fault. These thoughts hit her and seemed to laugh at her as these thoughts stayed in her head, bouncing around. She started crying. Her eyes started burning from a mixture of sobbing and not sleeping for 10 hours. Her arms gave out as she fell backwards, hitting the bed. She stared at the ceiling. She could see the outline of the fan swirling, evenly distributing cool air. Her eyelids went limp and fell shut.

In her dreams, Dylan's screams infected them, the electro-shock machine whirling. blind hot pain slowly consuming her, a mirror pointing out everything she didn't want to see.

"He needs you," one voice said.

"Dylan!" she screamed. Suddenly, the floor became a cold liquid. Rachel tried to move out of this liquid. She took a few steps forward, water sloshing like a blender around her feet. She took about maybe five steps forward before falling to her knees crying. Suddenly, the ground became soft with grass. A stray bird took off next to her, Then, she heard the song of execution, a mixture of organ and bells, as sobs the air filled around her.

Whose execution was she at? Was it her own? Maybe it was a family member—or maybe Maxton or Dylan. The thought of death made Rachel want to sink to her knees. That's what a lot of people saw: death, a horrifying enigma that would take you in its grasp and yank you away from family and friends. Maybe your death would be violent or just a peaceful process, and you'd be able to wave goodbye to your friends and family. Rachel heard fabric being twisted as she heard Dylan's voice.

"You've thrown so much shit at me that death probably will be the easiest task so far."

Rachel ran towards the voice, screaming his name. That's when she heard the first crack, like a rock hitting a tree, and she heard Dylan's scream—not his angered scream but a deep scream letting out all of the air in his lungs. She suddenly heard his voice stop calling for help.

Rachel moved slowly, not wanting to believe what sounds were unfolding in front of her.

"Dylan," she breathed, as her heart and mind sank into the darkness of her mind. All of a sudden, she was awake. She couldn't breathe. She couldn't think or move. She was wrapped around in a blanket.

"Mom!" she called out. Her voice was hoarse and raspy. She wanted some sort of comfort that a parent could provide. She hated her dreams. Suddenly, that made Rachel stop and think about what she did not hate about herself. She hated the way she cried, her family, and her dreams, or was she just moody teenager going through the beauty of hormones? Either way, this sucked.

Rachel climbed out of bed, her arm aching and having fallen asleep. She moved her arm back and forth.

"Mom!" she called out, taking a few steps forward. Her heart pounded. What if they were dead? Rachel worried, would their deaths be her fault? She pressed on the door, and it flung open.

"Rachel! Heavens! What are you doing awake? It's 2:00 A.M.!" her mother replied.

"I had a nightmare," Rachel whispered, flinching with each word.

"Screamed for too long?" her father's voice asked, slightly vibrating the room.

Rachel nodded before taking a few steps forward.

"Do you want to lay down with us?" her mother asked, patting the bed. Rachel nodded, feeling silly for doing this, but she needed the comfort of a parent.

After about four hours of trying to sleep, Rachel gave up and headed to school early. She needed to apologize to Maxton, even if he didn't want to talk to her.

Rachel walked out of her neighborhood to where she knew the school was. They were in tenth grade, so there were two more years before graduating and getting out of Richvill.

"Maxton?" Rachel called out. No response. Of course, he wouldn't want to talk to her, but she still needed to apologize. Wait. No, he should apologize to her. She tried to help him in the only way she knew how!

"Maxton!" she called out. Her voice shook the school violently.

"What?!" Maxton replied, angry. He hated when she screamed.

"I'm sorry about what happened at church—" Rachel started but was cut off.

"It doesn't matter!" Maxton replied, walking away. Rachel followed his footsteps.

"Yes, it does! I shouldn't have done that. And I'm probably going to hell for it," she replied.

"I don't care about the church incident. I was just pissed off and tired! I really don't care, and you're not going to hell. I am." He mumbled the last part thankfully. In Richvill, going to hell could be justified for thousands of reasons—like lying, getting angry, slamming the door, basically any annoying thing, and you were going to hell.

Awkward silence seemed like a deadly disease.

After school, Rachel told Maxton a plan she had. It was a stupid plan, but it was still a plan. She would try and sneak into the church, but she would need some help from the outside.

"Rachel, you're crazy," Maxton told her but then added, "But, damn! Sure, I'll help."

The plan was that, at 4 o'clock, Maxton would go into the confession stand, and while Maxton created a distraction, Rachel would climb under one of the seats and do her best to record a session. Setting the camera up was Maxton's job. Hopefully, he could get that done.

2:30 Two hours until go time.

Rachel was sitting in her room perfectly still, like a game of statue. Every breath made her shake. She held her eyes closed for a few moments before waiting for her computer to read the message. The code word X meant "go time." She was shaking. This was the first illegal thing she had ever done. Technically, the posters had been illegal, but no one seemed to notice those. Maybe no one cared to figure out who put the posters up. Probably everyone saw them but just weren't sure who, and didn't see the posters as a threat, but what Rachel was doing next would be seen as a grade 500 threat.

She was glad to have her voice back but was too anxious to use her voice. She packed her bag with as many things she could fit in her purse. She was going to be there until the morning, recording and listening to everything. Could she handle this again? Probably now. Did she really care what she could handle at this point?

No! She wanted something to happen, and as a revolutionary, she would be forced into a lot of uncomfortable positions. Rachel sat there, anxious about every life decision. Maybe she could cancel this plan. No. She'd taken too many steps forward. She refused to take any steps backwards.

1 hour until show time.

Rachel felt her hands too clammy and started shaking back and forth. She pressed them against her lap to steady herself. Then, she let out a heavy sigh. She wanted to run away. She didn't, though. She stood up, pacing back and forth. She waited for any sign from Maxton. If he was at the church, would conjuring a keyboard even work?

What if she missed her signal?

These were the thoughts going through her head, instead of one thought. For a time, they seemed to roll down like tumble weeds. Suddenly, her heart started pounding like a flame. Is that what made the Amazon Desert? Is this how people felt when they heard about it, like the world was ending? Rachel leaned against her bed, as she was starting to get impatient. Her mind seemed to convince her that she was going to die. She let out a shaky breath.

"I can handle this," she whispered, pulling in her knees. She stayed in this position as she noticed a slight vibration on her arm. She pulled up the keyboard and heard the word.

"X." Rachel nodded before grabbing her cane and sneaking out of the house. She heard the vroom of cars and horns of drunk or high drivers. She sighed and let her body relax against her own guilt. She would call down the fall of Richvill—to hell with the guilt! Rachel pushed the door open, closing in, and hiding under the seats. Her heart pounded as she let the rug gently cover her. She heard footsteps pass by. Were they Maxton's or Dylan's? She hoped they were Dylan's, so badly!

Rachel heard the sound of a book hitting someone's head. The boy screamed. Rachel felt her limbs contract and her heart rate speed up. She waited for something to happen, some kind of sign. She felt her body tense up. She closed her eyes, even though she didn't see anything. Maybe if she ignored it, it would go away, but the boy's screams were longer this time. Then, the cracking of skin against a book stopped.

The preacher started to shout about trauma and started making the kids read their sexual fantasies. Rachel felt herself blushing. She heard a lot about people pinning another person against the walls, beds, lockers—various locations. A lot of it, Rachel blocked out—until she heard one voice she recognized—a stuttering voice, soft and gentle.

"I was p-pinned against the wall. He pulled me closer...then I-" Dylan started, and then Rachel heard him let out a startled scream.

"What was that?" Rachel hardly whispered that. Her voice was worried, and she needed to figure out what that sound was. Then, she heard a water bottle, and Dylan complained about being all wet, as another thought went through Rachel's head. Put a bunch of gay kids in a room with other kids and boom-chick-a-boom! They're straight. Rachel touched her hand to her palm.

The rest of the day, she heard kids being shocked—sobbing, begging for parents. Rachel rocked back and forth very slightly, her knees to her chest, and her mind took a deep plunge.

What would happen if she got caught? What would happen to *her*?

If she got caught, she'd be arrested, point blank, but maybe there was a way around this. Rachel would have to get her group of rebels together sooner rather than later. She sat under that church bench, counting every second. She lost track about three times, then suddenly silence wound around her like a possessed doll, eerie silence—no wave of relief washing over her, just a sense of uneasiness. Was every kid in the church killed while Rachel dozed off? ...if she even did? She felt the sour taste of uncertainty in her mouth, as she made a face at it. She hated this feeling. Who knew what would happen? Rachel's heart was unsteady as she felt herself doze off.

Chapter eight. You know that feeling that the world's ending? Well, for Rachel, it may be. Do revolutionaries have to go to school?

Rachel wasn't sure what time she woke up or what time it was when she did. She moved awkwardly, pinching her lips. Her back hurt, same with her hip. Suddenly, she heard footsteps heading towards her. When the footsteps got closer, she pulled herself against the wooden bench.

She heard the person bend down as she expected something to happen.

"Rachel?" She heard Dylan ask. He touched her hand. Rachel's first instinct was to pull away, but she let him rub a hand over her shoulder.

"Dylan," she whispered.

"What are you doing here? You're straight. At least, I think so. Maybe you're bi," he whispered to her. Rachel shook her head, before yanking Dylan down under the bench with her.

"I'm going to start a rebellion," she told him. Rachel heard him gasp. He slowly moved to her, hugging her. They stayed under that bench, and the position looked really wrong, Dylan had his head on her shoulder. She had her arms around him. His hand rested on her upper back. She had her arms wrapped around his neck.

"You need to get out of here," Dylan whispered, pulling away.

Rachel shook her head, holding Dylan's hand.

"I'm not leaving without you," she told him, feeling cliche for saying that phrase, used in almost every action book or movie, but her tone was serious. She held onto the tension of the air, projecting the tension in her voice. She moved her hand awkwardly onto her lap, sitting up slightly. She rested her hand on his and said, "Dylan, please! We can leave together." She begged. She missed him; so did Maxton. Maxton wanted Dylan to know he needed to see him. She felt Dylan look away from her. She felt a new emotion reveal itself. Her throat was sore.

She felt Dylan grab her hand and put it to his cheek, shaking his head gently.

"Rachel. listen. I'm going to be released soon. I guess they think it's working. If you're caught, they'll kill you," he told her, pushing Rachel slightly.

Rachel grabbed his hand, slowly closing her fingers around his. She whispered,

"Dylan, I'm more than willing to die. You should know that."

"Rachel, we all need you alive. The rebellion needs a spark—you're that spark," he said, pressing down on the set of her collarbone. Rachel ended up squeezing his hand.

"Rachel. Go," Dylan told her.

Rage slowly coated her throat, as Rachel held onto one hand, about to yell at him. She pulled away. She could feel his fear pulling on her, begging for her to leave. She felt her heart fold over as guilt yanked on her, making her want to give in. until she finally said this.

"I'll leave--only if you stay safe," she told him.

"Deal," he muttered, before grabbing her hand and taking her out of the church. She slowly made her way to the house. Her excuse would be that she fell asleep at Maxton's house. His parents were never home, so it didn't matter. She felt for her keys. Opening the door, warm air blew against her cold frame. Rachel took one step in.

"Mom, Dad?" she called out. No response, only silence. They were probably asleep. Rachel was happy about that. Why would they just go to sleep? Maybe Maxton called them? That's the most likely situation.

She navigated her way to her bed. She didn't want to go to school but had no choice. she was socially exhausted. If she had one more ounce of info forced into her brain, she would scream. She went into her room and put her uniform on and headed back to school.

Suddenly, while Rachel was sitting in first hour, a new teacher came. Her voice was oddly robotic, and a robotic screech would whine any time she moved. The sound annoyed Rachel. *Where was Mr. Kugar?* Rachel raised her hand.

"Yes, girl with curly blonde hair?" The teacher's voice was almost robotic.

"Where's Mr. Kugar?" Rachel asked.

"He was taken away for government purposes," the robot teacher responded. Rachel let that sink in.

Suddenly, she realized that Mr. Kugar wasn't homophobic. He did something against the government, and they were doing who knows what to him! Rachel felt the tension in the air increase. She tried to spear her throat to interrupt the silence, but her attempts were futile. She sunk her head down against her desk for a second. Then, suddenly, she felt a metal hand SLAM against the back of her head. Her head erupted in agony as she felt a shooting pain in her neck.

"Do not go to sleep," the robotic teacher told her. "And open your eyes," she added.

Rachel was angry and yelled, "I'm blind! In public, I close my eyes, because I'm told they look weird," Rachel replied.

The teacher didn't seem to care and whirled back and forth. Rachel awkwardly switched around to face the robotic teacher. It was going to be a long year. Rachel could feel it in her gut. Thankfully, there were just two more weeks until summer break, and then she was free, unless…

…her dad made her work at the small diner that hardly anyone knew existed. She would love not to be seen until August 19th. Rachel moved awkwardly in her seat. By the time class was over, she was way too tense to relax. She moved her cane across the floor and into hallway and climbed into the desk of Ms. Jackie's rooms. She waited for the familiar sound of the teacher's voice to start the lesson and was relieved when that expectation was met. Maybe the school wasn't as different as she feared, or maybe it stayed the same with only a small amount of change. Was Rachel going to adjust? She laid her head on her arms, thinking about change. Was the school going to be rebuilt? Rachel hardly needed her cane at school, but if it was rebuilt, could she readjust? She didn't want to think about that. The town was built on memories—and maybe dead bodies. Was Richvill homophobic from the moment the small town came into existence? That was a good question. Rachel let out a soft sigh and ran her hand down her neck.

"Hey, Rachie?" Maxton said. As he sat down, the chair squeaked and whined from the sudden weight. Rachel touched his shoulder.

"Hey," she said. He held her shoulders, so he knew she was listening.

"Dylan?" he asked, not asking her about the conversation therapy.

"No," Rachel shook her head and sighed. Damn it! She was exhausted. The skin under her eyes burned but felt better since she closed them. She was going to stay awake longer. Maybe she could start a small amount of gasoline, and the town would light the rest on fire. That was the only way to get this hell to stop. She could reset some of the damage, but like an actual flame, no matter how you remodeled and repair, there would always be a spark of fear that was hidden in the frame.

Finally, one thought hit her like a sock full of

mud, which wasn't as painful as it sounded. Just trust her when she imagined that.

"When will he be better?" Maxton asked.

"Soon. He's progressing. He was able to sit up," Rachel explained. It was code. He was the same old Dylan, just probably traumatized, and would have third degree burns all over his body. Rachel smiled but squeezed Maxton's hand, saying, "Sorry." She felt Maxton sigh. He missed his boyfriend, and Rachel missed her other brother. Dylan was seven days older than she was, so they were both part of a weird "family." They had lost their one family member--their father (Von). They created a whole backstory for their "family." In their "family," their mother left, and Rachel and Dylan were twins, even though Rachel really didn't know what he looked like. Did appearances really matter when the person treated you like you are a teenager and independent?

No, it didn't matter.

Rachel snapped back into reality, letting out a shocked sound like a scared kitten.

"Are you okay?" Maxton asked her, touching her arm.

"Yes. I'm fine," she lied. Her mind was being a jerk again, like anyone's. She wanted to sleep for a long time, and maybe just suddenly not know about the world outside her dreams, but not now. If she ran away now, she'd be a coward. She hated calling herself a coward.

"Shit, I'm tired," Maxton whined, leaning back in his chair. Rachel was, too, but she didn't say anything until she did.

"Yeah," she replied. Why wasn't the class starting? She gave up and fell asleep, her head on her hands. She woke up with a stiff neck and arms, and she felt her eyes not hurting as much. Maxton's hand was on her shoulder. Rachel jumped, startled.

"Sorry, Rachie. Class is over. I wanted to wake you up. The class had free time. You didn't miss squat," he told her calmly.

"Thanks," she replied, using her other hand to push up herself up. Maxton walked with her to their next class. Class was boring as ever, so much mindless activity to the point where Rachel couldn't tell whether the school was real or a dream. All she knew was it was lunch time, and she was hungry. When she got her tray, the tray told her what everything was, if she waved her hand over the food item. This made eating a lot easier. A slight vibration echoed against her skull. She leaned forward, waiting for this weird sensation to stop. She pinched her nose as this sensation got stronger. She didn't like it—not at all.

"Rachie?" Maxton asked, holding her hand. She didn't respond to this. He tried to squeeze her hand, but Rachel let out a muffled, startled sound. Suddenly, Rachel felt the sensation fade. Maxton's hand was around her wrist. She squeezed back.

"What was that?" Maxton asked.

"Don't know, nor do I really care," Rachel replied, touching the back of her head, combing a finger through her curly hair. "It felt like my head was going to explode," Rachel explained, still rubbing her head

Maxton hugged her but then proceeded to let go of her.

"Where are you going during the summer?" he asked.

"I'm out of town... working," she explained, giving Maxton a suspicious look, like he hit a nerve.

"Gee, sorry! You don't need to look at me like that," Maxton replied, moving away from Rachel.

"Sorry. It's just that you never ask."

"I forget to," Maxton said. There was a silence between the two. Then, suddenly, they both broke out laughing. They couldn't stop.

"You always forget," she said, slapping

Maxton on the back a little harder than she intended. He let out a muffled sound from her hand.

"Sorry," she replied.

"It's fine," Maxton replied. A smile could be heard in his voice. Finally, lunch was over, and Rachel still couldn't stop laughing. People thought she was high. She explained, but the people she told didn't find Maxton forgetting to ask her a question funny. That was because they didn't know Maxton, the way Rachel knew Maxton. All they saw was the shy quiet side of him, the always-smiling side of him. They didn't know how he acted behind that, or the fact that, when bored, he one time put a pencil in his mouth and ran around Rachel's house, screaming, "I'm a walrus!" That was an interesting event, and even her parents thought this child was insane, but it was all in good fun. Rachel would have to explain. Hell, she fully understood why Dylan loved Maxton. He was just lovable.

Chapter nine. Dylan's back, and he's in on the plan. Also, Rachel can be a jerk.

After school, Rachel felt a vibration against her hand and recognized the similar tone dial of a message. She pulled up her computer, making it read it aloud to her.

"Meet me in the woods at the first tree." She listened to this twice, just so she could remember, and she tried to walk out, but then, her mom stopped her.

"Where have you been?! You never came home last night! Me and your father were worried sick about you!" she scolded.

Rachel kept her cool and said, "I was at Maxton's house. I fell asleep before I could send a message!"

"Where are you going now?" her mother asked, tapping her foot.

"Maxton wants to see me."

"Oh, well, if that's all, I'm ok with it. Just don't hang out with that fag boy. You and Maxton's relationship is good enough. You don't need any of that artificial stuff," she told Rachel, as Rachel uncomfortably moved her shoulder. She walked away and walked outside, then waited till she heard the door close and walked towards the woods.

She heard a loud whistle shoot out through every tree touching her ears. She repeated the whistle, making Dylan jump.

"There you are," he mumbled, grabbing her hand. His hand was freezing and shaking.

"Are you okay?" Rachel asked, rubbing a hand over Dylan's, which were strangely sweaty.

"Yeah, just a little spooked. I don't know why. I shouldn't be."

"It's okay," Maxton said. Rachel heard fabric scrunch and then Maxton's arm get pushed away.

"Sorry, Dyl, what's wrong?" Maxton tasked Dylan.

"I'm sorry. You scared me," he explained.

"You're like a jumpy cat," Maxton said and let out a soft laugh.

"I guess I am," Dylan replied. Rachel felt a slight undertone of guilt in Dylan's voice.

"Are sure you're okay?" Rachel asked again, her nerves now flaring up

"Yeah."

Awkward silence circled them slowly. Rachel was the first to break it.

"I'm skipping church on Sunday," she stated. Both of the boys made a sound in the backs of their throats.

"What?"

"I'm skipping church. If I spend one more second in there, I'm going to scream," she said, moving her arms up in an exasperated motion.

The two boys stared at Rachel as she held her arms covering her chest. She heard her own heartbeat.

Dylan moved his hands nervously before he spoke. "What? I mean this is Insane," he whispered

"They're using a religious source to excuse horrible things. They're using a misunderstood bible verse to run a town. This is brainwashing. The verse is so drilled into our minds. Think about it, Dylan."

Rachel stopped for a second, moving her hand into her hair. "When we go to church, we're told, 'do not have sexual relations with a man as one does with a woman; that is detestable ... If a man has sexual relations with a man as one does with a woman, both of them have done what is detestable. They are to be put to death; their blood will be on their own heads.' But there's more than that there! The forbidden pages! There has to be! I've listened to them. I used the girl—what was her name? J-Jemma! Yeah, we sat in the woods, and we read the WHOLE Bible."

"Wow," Dylan muttered.

"We're doing this," Maxton mumbled. He pulled on his sleeves.

"I'm going to publish the audio, Dylan, you know about it, right?" she asked.

"Mhm," he mumbled out loud.

The family reached forward, put their hands over each other, and shot their arms up. They were a team. They would be for the rest of their lives. It was what mattered most, Rachel smiled. It was nice having Dylan back.

Rachel headed home. She was getting angry by hearing vrooms of car horns yelling, cussing. There had to be more to this small town except cars, except yelling, except violence. If Rachel could escape this shit, she would run away and allow her mind to become her reality.

In her reality, Dylan and Maxton could be the cutest couple and be open about it. Maybe Von wouldn't have killed himself. People could just love one other. It wouldn't matter if you were a woman and a man, or a woman and a woman. Or a man and a man.

You could just love. That was Rachel's mind. She felt her legs ache with each step as she climbed into her house. Why didn't she use a window? She could feel the open window and didn't feel like going in the door. She sat in her room, computer in front of her, as she hit the download button. She felt a vibration in her ear:

"Upload complete," the voice said.

Her heart was pounding as she muttered, "It's

done." She mumbled as a relieved sigh escaped her lips.

Rachel waited for about 10 to 15 minutes. When she felt a vibration on her leg, she tried to pull away, then realized she had her first comment, since this was so controversial.

She moved her finger and let it read the comment aloud.

"This is so fake! The faggots deserve it."

Rachel squeezed her pant leg. She felt her fingernail hit her skin. She shook back and forth, but she never said anything about it. She knew this would happen. Only one thought went through her head: *Don't let Dylan see this, if he sees this, it will push him off the edge. The kid doesn't need that to happen. He can't take another thing.* She pulled on her hair, waiting for her mind to get under her control.

She pressed on her face. She didn't scream, nor did she cry. All she did was allow the hard part of her wrist to sink into her useless sockets. She tensed up, allowing her throat to become tight. She slammed one hand against her head, a small thunk sounding against her. She slammed her wrist against her head again. Then, she stopped.

Why was she hurting herself? She was angry and had no way to vent, and her parents weren't home, so she punched a pillow a few times. Her head was on her knees. As she calmed down, she felt her hair tickle her knees. She waited for some sort of sound to catch her attention, but nothing did, except a vibration notifying her of every single responding message. She tried not to count them.

100, maybe 150? Nearly the whole town knew about this unknown video that was posted, and no one knew who posted it. Now, Flormorent was going to read it, and then soldiers would interview or torture all 200 of the town.

Rachel allowed a robotic voice to read out every comment. There were about 100 of them.

"The fags deserve it," one angry commenter repeated.

"How could someone do this?" One person asked. Rachel wondered the same thing.

It was 50/50, Rachel suddenly heard the tapping of soldiers' feet surround the streets. *Why were they marching?* she made her facial expression ask, but she already knew the answer. They wanted to know who made the video. Dylan knew it was up, but he just couldn't watch it.

Rachel felt the vibration of knocking as the reality of her having to open the door set in. She walked to the door.

"Do you know anything about this video?" A soldier tried to put a laptop to her eyes, but all Rachel saw was a bright light.

"No, sir! And I'm blind," she stated.

"Where are your parents?" Rachel was questioned.

"I honestly don't know," she said.

Then, she told him, and the solider swore under his breath. She shook her head and suddenly told him, "Hey, if you want information from me, you need to stop being an asshole."

Silence rung around them as Rachel pulled on the skin on her neck.

The door was slammed as she heard them depart, talking about how she probably did this, but they didn't have enough evidence and how she had a big mouth on her. After this happened, Rachel lay on the couch as another vibration in her made her pass out.

Rachel was standing in a field. An array of wheat and flowers whipped against her bare legs, back and forth. The air tasted sour, as if something bad was about to happen, Rachel took about 4 steps forward before hearing, no feeling the vibration of a bell. Then, she heard an organ play out a terrifying tune. She felt her mind start racing. What was going on?

"Dylan! Maxton!" she screamed. Her legs felt more like massive pieces of metal. No matter how she hard she tried to move, she couldn't.

She heard a scream, then a loud cracking. She heard a soft sob and then a moan. Then, silence. She wanted to find them. No, not want—she *had* to find them. They couldn't be dead. *They can't be dead!* Wind was beating against her. Her limbs were being forced every which way. She held onto nothing as her ears started ringing. She covered them. She used her foot as a cane. Every step she took, wind blew on her even harder. She was pushed backwards and fell, sprawled out on the ground. Suddenly, she felt cool metal forced against her forehead and a low growl of a voice.

"Now, we killed those fags. Why don't we take care of the one who started this rebellion?" the low growl of a man spoke. Suddenly, Rachel felt a burning sensation go through her forehead. She let out a strangled gasp.

Rachel couldn't feel anything—no emotion, and she couldn't feel the ground under her or her own breath. Where was she? Suddenly, she tasted it—the iron taste and smell of blood. She tried to move her hand to wipe the blood away, but she couldn't move her arms. Then, the blood taste stopped. She heard someone but couldn't make out what they were saying, and then, there was just darkness.

Rachel sprung up, hyperventilating. She was in a cold sweat. Her hair stuck to her shoulders and chest. She took a deep breath, afraid to move or look up. Her whole body was now shaking. She couldn't breathe or handle this all at the same time. She tried to feel where she was. She reached one arm out, and the arm hit the ground. She was on the couch. Why was she so scared? That dream... her whole body tingled, as she pulled up her video and listened to the comment. There was a war going on...Because of her on the internet, there were death threats and the start of anger, people rising up. On the internet, you were anonymous. It was against the law for them to track you. It violated the act of privacy, which happened in 2026.

Rachel felt her heart pound. not because she was scared... no, because she was excited. She had about 100 people on her side, and there were only 100 people on the opposite side. including soldiers. If a war broke out, there would be equal ground on each side. Suddenly. Rachel got an idea. She turned her video camera on but covered it with a piece of duct tape.

She took a deep breath and then said everything she had been feeling in front of the camera. When she was done, she uploaded the video. She sat on the couch in silence for a few minutes. Rachel, a blind girl, was changing Richvill. Was it for the worse or for the better? That thought made Rachel think for a second. If Richvill was changing, how would it affect the world?

Change was a word everyone found terrifying, but in some cases, could change be good?

Chapter ten. A war is brewing. Dylan is coming back.

Dylan was lying on his back in his bedroom. He missed this. He missed his bed. Heck, he even missed his annoying little sister Kathrine, who was curled up next to Dylan. His appearance had changed. He had healed-over scars on his left and right arm. His hair had become a little darker and was completely brown, and his chest had scars from being shocked. His dark eyes didn't have the same light as they once did. Everything about him was different. He seemed so scared.

Kathrine also changed. Her red hair had been bleached down to blonde, with a blue tint. Her hair was straight instead of curly and extremely soft. The two half siblings were sleeping soundly. Occasionally, one of their legs would twitch, or one of them would roll over, or one would cuddle closer to the other. No one wanted to wake Dylan up, but suddenly, stomping feet caused him to jump and wake up. He pulled Kathrine closer to him. He wanted to protect her. Suddenly, he heard the door swing open. Wat was going on?!

"Mom? Dad?" Dylan called out. There was a soft yell back. He heard his mother's footsteps echo in the empty hallways.

"Hey, sweetie! Don't worry about them. They're just soldiers. Someone uploaded something. They might ask you some questions," she explained, smiling. Dylan felt warm tears build up in his eyes. Hs mother still loved him. She just couldn't show it in front of his father.

"Okay, Mom," Dylan replied, moving Kathrine into his lap. Her small chest was moving up and down. Dylan heard two people marching towards his room. He held onto Kathrine as the two soldiers entered the room.

"Do you know anything about the video uploaded?"

Dylan looked the soldiers over. One was a girl who was thin, and her skin was clear, revealing multiple wires and a red line that kept her jaw connected to her face. She made Dylan uncomfortable, so he looked away from her. The second soldier was a man with a large nose. He was muscular and had black hair, the polar opposer to his partner's white hair.

"No," Dylan replied, finally answering the robot woman's question.

"Why did it take you so long to finish?" she questioned.

"I just woke up, and I'm being questioned by a soldier at an unholy hour."

"True," the robot soldier replied as Dylan

squinted in the darkness. He saw a keyboard appear in front of him.

"Name?" the robotic solider asked.

"Dylan," he muttered.

In a second, she had ALL of his information.

"It says you are a faggot," the robotic voice boomed. Dylan tensed up and felt his breath exhilarate.

"I-I went to the church. I was cured!" He instantly replied. His heart was shaking, and his hands seemed to get clammy.

"You do understand what this means, correct?" The robotic solider had latched onto Dylan's wrist. He let out a strangled cry. This is what woke up Kathrine.

"Dylan?" she asked, sitting up on her elbow. Her little voice called out.

"It's okay, Kathy. Go back to sleep," he whispered. She was only half asleep, and she lay back down, already asleep.

"And your is boyfriend Maxton Oliver?" The male soldier asked, reaching into his pocket, pulling out a needle and forcing it into Dylan's arm.

Dylan felt like he couldn't control his body or words and just nodded. What were they doing to him? He felt two arms wrap their arms around his body and felt himself being moved. The reality began to set in for Dylan. They were taking him to be executed. He started whispering, "I don't wanna die. I don't wanna die!" to the point the phrase didn't sound like a phrase. Another thought went through Dylan's head.

"Even if you weren't drugged, they would have found out about Maxton eventually."

Dylan felt guilt rip him apart. he was going to die at 16.

He felt himself thrown into a vehicle and felt as a weight seemed to hold him in place. He felt tears falling down. He felt the car come to a halt. as the same thing that happened to him happened to Maxton. There was nothing neither of them could do. Suddenly, Dylan felt Maxton hold his hand.

Maxton looked at Dylan and whispered, "I love you." He had a sad smile plastered all over his face. He always had a brave face on for Dylan, no matter the situation.

Dylan whispered back, "I love you," then felt the drug that was injected into him take hold of his mind, causing him to pass out.

The car drove for another 30 minutes, before stopping at a grey building surrounded by wheat and flowers. A bell hung off the top that would ring with each teen/child killed. Maxton tried to hold Dylan but couldn't move. He squeezed his hand but realized Dylan was drugged.

"Baby, I'm right here," he mumbled before drugs took over his mind. The two boys' breaths were uneasy, and their hands in each other's hands. The male soldier set them in a room, with one bed hanging off the wall. The room looked like a solitary confinement cell. Maxton was in the room next to Dylan, as they both laid unconscious on their beds.

In Dylan's dreams, he and Maxton were in that forest. Suddenly, Dylan was sitting with his back against a tree. Then, Maxton pinned him against the tree as his lips pulled on Maxton's. Dylan pulled him closer, as it suddenly started raining. Both boys sat there, drenched in the rain, their lips not moving from the other. Maxton grabbed Dylan's hair, slightly tugging. He didn't want this moment to end. He held onto Maxton, rain beating against their bodies. They could be stupid teenagers. Finally, no one would ever come to the woods. They could have just stayed there forever. But that changed. About one month earlier, everything changed. It was May 12th, the worst day of Dylan's and Maxton's lives—those pictures! What if they didn't go into the woods that day? Would they have still been caught?

Dylan sprung up, his heart pounding, and his black eyes darted around like pieces of coal. His breath coming out in gasps, he pulled into a ball, crying. Where was he? Then, he remembered. Was Maxton dead already? Or would he spend the next five years in this tiny cell with no human contact? If he was lucky, maybe he'd end up starving to death. He pulled his hands up to his face and then sunk his fingernails into his palm as hard as he could. Dylan wasn't sure what he was doing, but he remembered he did this when he was upset or stressed. He felt a small amount of blood slip down his hand, and then that's when he stopped.

As he sat there, death wasn't as scary before. He had nearly died when he was attacked. If that darkness was the only thing he would see instead of a horrible future of not being able to love who he loved...society saying, "It's not okay to be who you are." He would rather die, anyway. It was that simple, but then he thought about something. If Rachel's rebellion worked, all of this could change. Suddenly, metal footsteps sounded through the empty halls, scaring Dylan. He tensed up. His eyes tried to find the source. He suddenly heard just a phrase, but this phrase made his heart pound.

"Brain spike Sunday."

Dylan raised an eyebrow, trying to act all calm around the guards, but he knew this was no use.

A few days later, Dylan let the fact that tomorrow he was going to die sink in. He accepted it, but Dylan felt some strange tension in the air, like it was hard to breathe. He kept hearing popping all around but wasn't sure what the sounds were. At first, they were small things, like less guards inside the building and any interactions were even shorter—or maybe each guard sounded so tired when they walked by. Why were they so tired?

"Damn rebels," a male guard breathed out, as he walked by Dylan's cell.

Suddenly, Dylan felt his heart beat a little faster. Rebels! It had worked! The rebellion worked! It was 50/50 against each other! Would his death turn more onto Rachel's side? What about his mother? Which side would she be on, the homophobic or people for the LGBTQ+ community? She would be for the LGBTQ, but his dad wouldn't let her. He was so controlling and abusive. She was scared of him. That was why she always did what he said.

Dylan stayed curled in a corner, holding his knees to his chest as he heard more popping. He heard yelling, all phrases unintelligible,

Dylan waited there for about a few more hours until he heard every yell. Then, suddenly, everything turned to nothing, except for a few shots. This was not the sound of death, not an eerie silence—just like a candle being put out, but another lighter was slowly moving towards the wick. Another spark, and the wick would be re-light, and a small thought rumbled around in Dylan's mind.

Would a death be the new spark or would there never be a spark again? His thoughts kept going from this to family, to Maxton and even his "twin," as he whispered under his breath, "Rachel. Sis, if there is another side, I'll see you there."

He pulled onto his knees as if there was a way he could stop this, but he felt trapped. He felt so stuck, nothing he could do would fix this. He couldn't do shit. He was helpless, and his mind was going to be destroyed. He thought, *Would you have memories if you're dead? If your mind has an iron spike in it. are you still you?* Dylan felt himself crying again. He hated how much he cried. Maybe Maxton was crying, too. Probably, there was only so much someone could handle until they their breaking point.

Maybe he's already dead. Dylan thought, numbly.

He was wrong with that thought. Maxton was very much alive and was also having these thoughts.

Dylan didn't want to die. He didn't want Maxton to die. He no longer cared if he died himself, but Maxton was scared of death. He always was. He always would be.

5:30am Richvill, Church of the Innocent.

Dylan felt his body being struck by the cold. Both of his hands were tied down. He couldn't move. He looked over everyone. The whole town was staring at him, everyone except his mother, sister, and Rachel. Rachel was crying.

Dylan looked at her and then said, "Hey, Rach. Don't cry." His voice was dry, and this didn't work. Rachel just cried harder. Nothing he said could fix this. Nothing he said could comfort her. He couldn't make her feel better.

More tears fell down her face as her helplessness spread across her face like a bone sticking out of the flesh. She let a sob escape her lips. Suddenly. Dylan looked at the red, carpeted, tall benches of the church one last time as he heard a voice from behind him.

"And finally, any last words, fag?"

Dylan slowly nodded, surprised he had this privilege of a last word.

"After all the shit this town has thrown at me, death will be the easiest thing to get past," he said, staring at the town. Suddenly, he felt his skull crack, and he let out a scream until he couldn't anymore. He couldn't breathe. Dylan's limbs went out of control. All at once, he just stopped moving. Blood was dripping out of head. His eyes were still full of terror, as he took one last breath. Then, he stopped.

Rachel started sobbing as his mother screamed.

Chapter eleven. Rachel's grief and the rebellion. Also, the crying person.

Rachel didn't need to see or have the ability to see to know that Dylan was dead. She felt her chest and heart being ripped out. She fell off the bench from sobbing so hard.

"Sweetie, don't cry for the faggot," her father told her. Finally, Rachel snapped. She yelled, "I'm goddamned blind! And I can see more clearly than most of you people—all one hundred and one of you here! How can you be so stupid?! YOU'RE ALL IDIOTS!" Rachel yelled as her tears fell down her cheeks, slowly hitting the carpet. Suddenly, she had another thought.

"Everyone tells me the church has a red carpet. Could the reason it is red be because of blood?" The thought made Rachel's stomach turn into a knot, in between crying and throwing up. She thought of something. She had lost all of her friends and her family in two weeks. She felt another half of her being broken—Dylan, her twin; Maxton, her twin's boyfriend, and Von. She lost them all, two to murder, and one to suicide.

She pulled her knees to her chest and started rocking while sobbing. She hugged herself. Everyone she loved was gone. She really didn't even care about her family. She felt two strong arms lift her up. She was crying too hard to fight against them, but she was soon loaded into the broken-down family van. The car was only used to go out of town, and they were only allowed to go out of town three times a year.

Rachel awkwardly asked through sobs, "Where are you taking me?" She asked her father through the sobs, gasping in between them.

"Cheering you up. Dylan deserved every

ounce of pain," her father explained before the white mini-van coughed and sputtered, then slowly puttered down the streets. Rachel made herself calm down, although a hard, burning knot stayed in her throat. *Where were they going?* Suddenly, Rachel heard the radio. It was playing an old song. She couldn't remember the name, but she listened to the words.

"You don't wanna be like me, kid! You don't wanna be like me, kid. You don't wanna look like me, kid. You don't want to see the things I've seen. You, don't wanna be like me." The singer seemed sad, as Rachel tried to figure out what the song was called, and when she finally remembered, the thought hit her in the head like a baseball. The song came out in 2020; it was called, *You Don't Wanna be Like Me, Kid*. Such an old song. Suddenly, Rachel had this strange thought.

Dylan's not dead. He's probably just sick or at conversation therapy. He's not dead. Rachel tried to convince herself, forcing herself into her own delusion. Was she losing her mind? No, she just was a sixteen-year-old that had lost way too much in only two weeks. She was now being forced to move on, way too quickly. This girl needed a hug, if she'd even let you—she was too angry for much of anything. but if someone could, she would have appreciated that.

The van rolled to a stop in front of a one-story diner, with grey bricks and a huge sign pointing directly to it, flashing red. The color red would stimulate appetite, and that's what this diner did.

Rachel didn't know this at the time, but her first act of defiance had been noticed, and it was spreading far beyond Richvill. Rachel was helped outside the car and led into the building. She sat down at the table, pulling herself upwards so her arms rested on the table. She heard the sound of meat frying and dishes being washed, until she softly heard a voice of someone.

"I'm sorry, Papa!" they begged.

Rachel didn't recognize the voices, but she still listened, because one, she had no choice, and two, because she was curious. She leaned back and heard the gruff voice of an old man.

"And you still watched it?!"

"I said I was sorry! Papa!" the other person begged. They had a voice that made Rachel feel bad, because they were so desperate.

"You aren't being a part of this! What happens in Richvill stays in Richvill."

"No, Papa. Listen, it isn't Just Richvill. It's the whole country of Sema!"

"You mean Oklahoma. It was called that before Flormorent took over. You remember that, June! Well, do you?!" he screamed, breaking a glass cup. Rachel tensed up, startled by the glass breaking.

"Yes, Papa, I do remember. It's just that I want Flormorent gone! And that change is going to stop with me!" June yelled.

Rachel felt a slight smirk build on her lips, even though her brain screamed at herself for doing this. She felt hopeful again. Maybe she and June could convince others to rise up.

"Go get what the people at the first table ordered," June's father instructed.

"Yes, Papa!" June said, as they walked out of the kitchen, stopping in-front of Rachel's table. June had green hair tied in a small bun They wore a skirt with a black shirt and had a white apron over it.

"Hi, I'm Ju- Jordan, and I will be taking your order," they said happily, before looking at Rachel.

"And, young one, would you like a Braille menu?"

"Yes, please. Thank you, Jordan," Rachel

replied.

Jordan gave a quick, "My pleasure," and then went to go retrieve the menu. Rachel stood quietly. Her legs started swaying back and forth. She felt awkward and uncomfortable. Suddenly, Jordan came back with the menu, setting the menu in front of Rachel.

"The menu is right in front of you. Can I get you some drinks?"

Rachel sighed and rubbed her finger over the Braille, reading. She wasn't hungry. She didn't feel anything, just a huge pit in her stomach, sucking away her appetite. She chose some lemonade. She told Jordan that, who gave her a quick smile.

"The lemonade will be out in just a few minutes," Jordan informed, slightly tapping Rachel's head. Rachel smiled. She liked Jordan. Maybe they could become friends.

But Rachel didn't really want friends, not yet, at least. However, maybe Jordan was different. This set Rachel's mind to go a million miles an hour,

Jordan's footsteps sounded as they set the drink down.

"Okay, so you guys from CornWell?" Jordan asked.

"No, Richvill," Rachel replied, wishing she didn't know about Richvill.

"Oh, it's a shame what happened there," Jordan answered.

Rachel felt the cold glass of lemonade, and she took the first sip, tasting the bittersweet taste of lemon. She finished the drink before Jordan came with the food, Rachel couldn't eat much of anything. She held the fork, but no matter how long she smelled the food, she couldn't eat. Her stomach was a like block of ice, and no matter how hungry she was, that ice wouldn't melt. Rachel sighed.

"Rachel darling, aren't you hungry? You

haven't eaten at all."

"No, I'm not eating," she whispered, turning her body away from her parents' voices, then away from the plate.

"Rachel, if you're still upset about Dyl-"

"I am," she mumbled and stayed with her arms pulled around her, as if she were in a straitjacket, but these days, straitjackets weren't used anymore. Now, you just were extremely sedated.

"Rachel, we didn't raise a rebel. We raised a porcelain doll. You'd be perfect for men, even though you're a little slow," her father said.

Rachel went silent; she was so angry. Could her parents make her feel any worse today, without intending to? Well, if they tried, they could, but they didn't mean to and still were. A horrible feeling of tension circled Rachel, like a tornado crashing against her body. She tensed up and moved her head to the side, and that's when she heard footsteps.

Suddenly, there was a crashing sound, Rachel felt for her cane, grabbing it. Then, she tapped back and forth, until she felt the jagged glass of a broken coffee mug.

"Here, let me help you!" she exclaimed, dropping her cane, and sitting on her knees as the hot coffee burned her legs.

"No miss, I've got this." Jordan said.

"Nope! I'm helping," Rachel replied, feeling over the jagged glass, holding onto each piece for a second or two, and then moving each one into a middle pile on the middle of the floor, with the pieces of the coffee mug clumped together. Jordan smiled at Rachel as they helped scoop up the rest in a dustpan. Bigger stores out of Sema had robots who would do this, but now Sema was at the bottom financially. The place used to be at the top of the top financially. Then, they fell down.

"Did we get all of it?" Rachel asked.

"Yeah," Jordan replied, helping Rachel up from her knees. For maybe a second, they held hands, but the two quickly pulled away from each other. Jordan moved their hands to Rachel's shoulders, helping her to her seat and helping her sit down.

"Sir, I am so sorry! I will go get you another cup of coffee shortly," Jordan said, then running off to get more. Rachel rapped her feet against the floor and still had sinking quilt that was choking her.

She wanted to go home desperately, if she had to be honest. She wanted to leave the dinner and go back to her home. She just didn't want to go home to Richvill—maybe CornWell wasn't that bad. Rachel thought to herself but then pushed that thought aside. The more she tried to explore into that thinking, something hit Rachel. She thought for a second. She knew for a fact that this feeling would be the same if she were in CornWell. Then, another thought came to her mind.

"Walking out of church." Maybe she could use online again, and her actions could be nationalized.

Rachel pulled out a small brail keyboard on her lap and started typing. She posted her idea and hoped that people cared enough about the cause to risk their lives. She didn't want that to happen, though, because she couldn't handle more death. She felt her head fall forward. She was emotionally drained.

"Rachel, are you okay?" her dad asked, while taking a bite out of his sandwich.

"It's nothing. Just leave me alone," Rachel mumbled, pulling her legs to her chest. She waited there for maybe about 10 minutes, waiting for something to happen. Suddenly, there was a small pop. Rachel raised an eyebrow at this, and why did it sound so much like gunshots? Then, Rachel heard another pop, and she slowly sunk further into her chair. Who was being shot at?

"Again?" Jordan whispered, with a small amount of urgency in their voice.

"What's going on?" Rachel asked.

"Nothing to worry about. They're just getting rid of any sort of rebellion activity before it has a chance to start."

"Oh, okay," Rachel said, nervously bouncing her leg. *What if they knew?* Would she be killed like Dylan.? The answer was no to both. No one in the government suspected a blind girl to start a rebellion. Everyone only saw her as her disability, but this was going to change very soon. Rachel was treated like a child, but after this week, she was going to be treated with respect for the first time and not seen as just a disabled girl who needed to be fed and guided. She was independent and strong. She would get the country of Sema to respect other people, even if it killed her—for Von, for Dylan and Maxton, for everyone who had been oppressed. She was going to let them have the feeling of being supported, and this journey would start on Sunday, after the family had finished their food at a diner. They headed to church.

Chapter twelve. The walkout and the rebellion.

Rachel sat in church, but in the middle of the service, she stood up and walked out. Suddenly, another person joined her until about a third of the 101 people had left, too. Two of these people were Dylan's mother and little sister.

Both of them had been so tired of all this, they didn't care how hard they would be hit. They didn't care how long their punishment would be, but if rising up would cause them to be axed down, so be it, people. Rachel didn't recognize that there was silence around them, and they weren't sure why.

Soldiers marched around the church in an attempt to detain the rebels, but the only way to detain them was to kill them all. The government had already killed half of the town's population. Were they ready to kill more? Rachel seemed to hear everyone's hearts' pounding in sync. They all knew the dangers of their actions. They knew this could kill them. They knew it all, but they still took the risk.

"For Maxton and Dylan," Rachel mumbled.

Someone caught onto what she said and yelled it, too. Suddenly, the whole crowd was yelling, "For Maxton and Dylan!" Then, someone added, "For Von!" Yells erupted around Rachel, as she felt tears slowly falling down. She was a spark to a candle, and this candle was called change. Suddenly, a loud pop broke the silence. Rachel tensed up.

Rachel heard more people. They were walking. A few were in cars. All at once, crowds of people circled around them, Rachel's body shook with anticipation. What would happen? Suddenly, another pop was heard from the opposite side, Rachel covered her ears. She heard screams full of pain, wanting something more then what Sema had to offer—all wanting for their kids to be accepted.

Rachel relaxed, taking a deep breath, and finally said this, "A message for Flormorent!" She took a shaking breath. "We can end this right here, if you call off your men and surrender," Rachel proposed, throwing her hands in the air and grasping nothing.

She continued and said, "If you side with me, this town will be accepting of any sexual orientation or gender identity. Brain Spiking will stop. You won't lose any more of your children. Or, you could side with the government and live under oppression. If you do not surrender, I will personally make sure the whole country of Sema will rise against you."

Rachel completed, and then she heard a voice she recognized. The voice belonged to Jordan. They ran up to Rachel, their green hair bouncing with each motion of their body.

Rachel felt arms around her, wrapping her in a hug.

"Oh my god, you're so brave," Jordan whispered into her ear.

"Jordan, please let go of me, I need to continue," Rachel said, wiggling out of their grip. As wind slowly blew Rachel's hair, she stood there like a woman on a mission. Her pale blue eyes shone with some unfathomable emotion. She stood there as more people came up in their cars. There were now about 300 people on Rachel's side and only one hundred people not on her side.

"You are outnumbered. Surrender," Rachel said slowly, but she heard another person scream.

"For Dylan, Maxton and Von!" That was when the first gun shot from Rachel's side blew. She felt a new emotion of fear boil inside of her. She wanted this to remain peaceful, but it couldn't. Suddenly, multiple gun shots fired at once. Rachel heard screams from the opposite side. She couldn't move.

This should have stayed peaceful. Rachel's mind couldn't move off of that fact, but she then remembered they had ruthlessly killed. She felt a rush of adrenaline wash over her. She heard the violent sound of gun shots wrap around her. but one woman stood different, a long-haired, skinny, long-shouldered woman, Dylan's mother. She awkwardly moved between the war zones. Who did she support—her husband or a sixteen-year-old? Rachel sensed this tension and put a hand on Dylan's mother's shoulder.

"Darla, I know this is difficult, but you have to pick a side," Rachel said slowly, so that Dylan's mom could fully understand her. Rachel could hear her heartbeat over all of the violence as Dylan's mother held her hand. She slowly heard a whisper.

"For Dylan." Rachel felt a rush of shock flood over her, as violence erupted further, Rachel felt her body tense. Suddenly, she took a few steps forward. She was now in front of the crowd. A cold gust of air pushed Rachel's blonde hair.

She suddenly heard more cars, and there he was—Flormorent—see-through skin, eyes glowing a deep red that struck fear into anyone who saw them. He had a thin jaw with two bolts sticking out of it, and he was dressed in a suit. Soon, soldiers circled him, protectively.

"May I have an explanation of what is happening?" a robotic voice called out as the popping of his jaw silenced the crowd.

Rachel felt its robotic metal hold on her shoulders. She shook the hands off.

Someone called out in the crowd, "You're killing our children!"

"I am only trying to keep our society

balanced," Flormorent responded, turning his head, looking at Rachel and scanning her. over

"And, such a beautiful thing, trying to rebel against me!" He grabbed Rachel's cheeks, staring into her pale, blue eyes.

"Don't touch me," she said in a hoarse voice, turning her head to the side. The president made a disgusted sound in the back of his throat. He forced Rachel's head to the side. She made a nervous sound. With one slap, he could easily kill her. She felt her throat go numb and dry. Her fingers hung at her knees. She started shaking as she whispered one phrase, "If you kill me, you'll have 300 people on you in a second with guns and so much more shit that could easily outnumber you. Do you really want to kill me?"

Rachel felt herself being lifted up by her chin for a second. She felt weightless as she was thrown through the air. She felt herself instinctively curl into a ball. She hit the ground with a large thud and let out a gasp. The wind was knocked out of her, but she was back up the second. She got her second wind. She felt bruises building up all over her body and tensed up, pulling her body up. She felt people pushing her forward until she was in front of the president again. Her heart pounded as she felt 500 eyes on her.

"People of Richvill, either listen to me, or all of you and your children will be executed."

Rachel heard the terrified gasps of everyone. She fought back a gasp herself before coming up with her response.

"People of Richvill, this is the reason we need a change. If anyone tries to rise up, they are threatened with guns and violence."

Suddenly, a flood of people attacked Flormorent. There was screaming and gun shots, and one sick sizzle of the president's jaw being ripped off.

Rachel felt even more people circle around

her, pushing her away from the initial crowd. Why were they protecting her? Rachel heard the sound of a machine shutting down. That was the last sound she heard, and then she felt a weight against the back of her head, knocking her unconscious. She woke up three times before she completely recovered.

The first time she awoke, she tried to sit up but felt her stomach turn into an icy block. She felt that she wasn't in her own bed as the scent of death and depression hit her like a brick. She felt over her blanket until she heard a voice she recognized. It was Jordan.

"Hey, Rachel, are you okay?" they asked, holding her hand.

"My head hurts a lot," she explained to Jordan.

"You got hit in the head. It makes sense," Jordan told her to run a hand over the bandage covering Rachel's face. Then, Rachel blacked out again. When she woke up again, she asked for Dylan, forgetting he was gone. When she remembered, she asked for Maxton, but she was then hit with the harsh reality that he was dead, too. Once again, she passed out, this time from pain. She was unconscious for three days, at which time, she finally woke up.

"Rachel? Hey, sweetie, your parents want to see you," a nurse called, walking into the room

"I really don't want to see them," Rachel calmly said.

"Okay," the nurse said confusedly, narrowing her black eyes at Rachel before walking off, her heels clicking. Rachel rubbed her head. She felt a bandage wrapped around her like a hug but over her head. She tried to stand up, but thousands of machines seemed to go off beeping and screaming in the small room. Rachel covered her ears as a small ounce of pain shot up her arm. She rubbed her free hand down her arm, starting at her shoulder.

Nothing felt out of the ordinary until she got to the crook of her arm where a plastic device stuck straight out with a tube hanging from it.

"What the hell?" Rachel whispered, feeling this device in her arm until she realized she was in the hospital.

She heard someone run up to the room, and a male's voice called out, "Hey, Rachel Wait to you walk around. You're connected to a lot of machines and an IV. Don't panic. Here, let me help," he said. Rachel heard shoes clicking as he walked to her.

"Just let me do that." He suddenly grabbed the remote and turned on the news. Rachel's heart pounded as she heard this statement.

"On 6:30am, last Sunday, Rachel Piper, Darla Burr, and Kathrine Reynolds all walked out of church and started chanting for LGBTQ rights to be accepted in Richvill. At 7:00am, 100 people from CornWell pulled up in their cars and started chanting, the same thing. That was when Flormorent came. That was when we discovered that our Dear President was a robot created from, AA.12. We cannot get anyone from that company to speak to us. A riot subsequently broke out, and the people destroyed Flormorent. We are not sure how many were hurt or how many were killed. Despite this, on Monday May 30th, the Country of Sema had their first vote for the first time in 80 years! And the results are in—"

Rachel's eyes widened as her lips turned into an anxious frown.

"20% of the Richvill population voted against LGBTQ+ rights. 70% for, and on June 1st, all members of the LGBTQ+ community will have equal rights." Rachel stood there smiling, bouncing slightly.

Were they fully out of danger? Not yet.

20 years later...

A girl with black curly hair and white glasses, her dress slightly hanging off of the ledge, sat, looking at the cloudy sky. That was when she saw a white dot, after twelve days of clouds. The stars finally showed themselves.

Author's note.

I want to thank everyone, my mom, grandpa, grandma and dad, my editor Andrea Foster, all of everyone in Creative Quills, my friends, Henry, Alex, London, my drama teacher—I love you all!

I started this book in January, after the idea of two gay kids in a homophobic town came to me while taking my friend home. I pulled out my phone and started working on it, and everything just fell into place. Originally, the Town of Richvill wasn't even called anything. But then I got the idea to have the poorest town be called "Richvill," just for the heck of it, and, yes, Richvill is spelled without the *e* on purpose.

The reason I made Rachel's character was I wanted to make a strong character with a disability. Rachel's character was to be twins originally, but the more I planned, the more the twins fused into one character. Rachel originally had brown hair, but I changed it to blonde—I'm not sure why. I want to clear up any confusion here. Rachel isn't dead, and there will be a second book, and since there will be a second book, I'm going to tell you all a tiny bit about the characters, but all you will be getting is their names and ages.

- Jackie Reynolds age: 16
- Presley Ariba age: 14
- Bell Dize age: 19.

That's all you can know. You'll have to wait until the book comes out! So, since you know about the characters of the second book, I'll tell you more about the characters in this book. Dylan's name was originally going to be a placeholder, but the name stuck. I made up Maxton's character on the spot. And for the final time thank you for reading this book!

About the Author.

CJ Kennedy has been writing for as long as he can remember, from fanfics to his own original stories. He lives in Oklahoma City with his two dogs, Henry, a German Shepherd/Lab mix and Baby. a Terrier/Pit Mix.

When CJ isn't writing, he is drawing and uploading on Instagram under the name of *AlexanderMoonstone2.* When not on Instagram, he's on YouTube under the name Izzy the Lily. He is a big fan of musicals and listens to them constantly.

Made in the USA
Monee, IL
26 September 2024

66641448R00115